NORWEGIAN
Troll Tales
from

Trolls Remembering Norwa[y]

REVISED AND EXPANDED

Retold by Joanne Asala
Including Illustrations by Theodor Kittelsen

Penfield
BOOKS

Dedication:

For my grandfather, Lon P. Dawson,
who taught me to love critters and creatures and things
that go bump in the night.

Joanne Asala received her degree in medieval English literature from the University of Iowa. She has edited several collections of Scandinavian, Celtic, and Eastern European folklore.

Acknowledgments: A special thank you to Darrell Henning, former director, and Carol Hasvold, librarian/registrar, Vesterheim, The Norwegian-American Museum, for use of their collection of historic Norwegian books and for help with the manuscript; Nasjonalgalleriet, Oslo, Norway, for many of the illustrations; Dreyer Forlag, Oslo, Norway, for use of their illustrations; Scott Winner, Little Norway, Blue Mounds, Wisconsin; Open House Imports; Bergquist Imports, Inc.; and Michael Feeney, the Mount Horeb troll carver.

Editorial Associates: Dorothy Crum, Melinda Bradnan, Maureen Patterson, Joan Liffring-Zug Bourret and Whitney Pope.

Graphics: M.A. Cook Design, Aaron Cruse Drawings by Diane Heusinkveld

Books by Mail
Norwegian Troll Tales
This book: $14.95, shipping $6.95
www.penfieldbooks.com
Penfield Books
215 Brown Street
Iowa City, Iowa 52245

ISBN: 1-932043-10-1
Library of Congress Control Number: 2005928535

Scott Winner at Little Norway, Blue Mounds, Wisconsin stands by trolls carved by Michael Feeney of nearby Mount Horeb. Michael denies responsibility for the naughty actions of any of his trolls.

Manufactured by Thomson-Shore, Dexter, MI (USA); RMA596MS242, July 2014

Contents

PART TWO: *The New World*

Vinje as the Root of a Pine Tree
ARTIST: *Theodor Kittelsen*

PART ONE: *The Old World*

The Troll Who Wonders About His Age
ARTIST: *Theodor Kittelsen*

The Old World Trolls of Norway

In the days now long departed, so far back that no one can quite say when, the trolls came to the land of Norway.

According to the most ancient of Norse myths, when the Earth was created from the fallen body of the giant Ymir, the maggots which emerged from his corpse were transformed by magic into the light elves and dark elves. Most of the trolls belong among the ranks of the dark beings, keeping to themselves in the damp bowels beneath the Earth's surface, plotting revenge and mischief against the sons of man.

When my grandmother and her family emigrated from Norway around the turn of the century, they brought with them a host of stories about the "Old Country." I remember sitting on Grandma's lap as a young girl, listening to her spin stories of fierce dragons and enchanted bears, of handsome princes and hideous giants, of clever foxes and ignorant peasants, of sorcerers and Vikings. But my favorite stories of all were about the trolls!

Grandma always had a good troll story waiting. She could tell me funny stories to cheer me up when I was feeling blue, or sad stories that would make me cry. When I was being particularly naughty, she would tell me the frightening legend of the troll who captured and ate wicked little girls. I would lie awake in bed, trembling and fearful, the covers pulled way up over my head, promising that I would behave better next time and praying that this Norwegian bogeyman wouldn't get me.

There are many kinds of trolls in Norway, according to my grandmother. Some are dour and ugly and grotesque in form, while others can be deceptively beautiful. The Huldre Troll, for example, is often breathtaking to behold. But one has only to look closely at her to see a cow's tail or goat's hooves peeking below her dress; or else the Huldre will be hollow when viewed from behind, proving that her beauty is only a shell.

Trolls in general are a mean lot, skilled at thievery and robbing humans of everything they hold dear—including their children. They seem to live only to cause hardship and grief to others.

Most trolls move about only at night, for sunlight is fatal to them. They fear the sunlight more than anything else and here is why: the sun's rays can turn a troll into stone! In Christian mythology, the trolls and other elves are really fallen angels, or pagans who had died and who were not quite good enough for heaven nor wicked enough for hell. They were stuck roaming the earth, and because the daylight world scorned them they were forced to keep to their caves until sunset. Many of the mountains of Norway are said to really be trolls who were accidentally caught in the sun's rays. But as the seasons turn, and the days grow short, the trolls have more time to cause trouble.

The reason why trolls hate people so much is that they look at them as invaders. Nowadays Norway is only covered in snow for six months of the year, but for thousands of years a giant glacier rested over the country, stretching from one end to the other. When the ice and snow had finally melted away, the trolls were the first ones there.

When the glacier retreated, human tribes from the south moved into the newly uncovered territory and named it Norway. They considered themselves the first inhabitants, but they soon discovered they were wrong. The trolls believed that everything surrounding their home belonged to them, including trees, rivers, farms and even churches—although they dared not set foot in those. They hated it when men cleared forests and planted crops. They found a hundred little ways to torment people; they might tangle their hair while they slept or tie knots in the tails of their horses. Or perhaps they would cause their cheese to go sour or their pots to spring leaks. They especially liked careless and lazy people, because they were easiest to play jokes on.

But occasionally you can find a good troll, one you can trust, who is actually friendly. The Nisse is just such a creature.

The Nisse is most often referred to as the Julenisse, the Christmas Elf. He likes human company, although he is rarely seen, and can typically be found on the farm. Recently there have been several undocumented reports of city-sightings.

The Nisse loves animals of all kinds, and if you are lucky enough to have one living in your barn, you need not worry about your animals becoming sick or getting stolen. Although he is generally mild in nature, the Nisse has been known to discourage would-be cattle thieves. Those animals under his protection are usually the sleekest and healthiest livestock around. People who stay in the Nisse's good graces, respect his privacy, and those who are kind to him often have good luck in return.

To keep the Nisse happy, the Norwegian farm wife will cook a special porridge known as *Rømmegrøt* and place it in the barn. Norwegian Christmas cards often depict this happy scene, neglecting to mention the fact that the Nisse has his origins as a heathen house god.

But for every good troll there are a dozen wicked types. The fjords are considered by some to be bottomless, and home to the Nøkk. In the vast oceans dwell the Draug, while the Risse-Gubbe live in the forests and the Fjell-Troll live in the mountains.

Some trolls are skilled musicians. In fact, many of the most widely known Norwegian songs and ballads were first played on a troll's fiddle, and many of the finest players learned their art from the Fossegrim.

Fossegrim is the most accomplished musician of the Troll family; he is the troll that makes his dwelling behind waterfalls. You can be looking right at a Fossegrim and never even know it. His body blends in well with the sparkling, moonlit, silvery water of the falls. He is almost never without his violin, and even if he were starving he would not trade it for a loaf of bread; but he is willing to share his talent with others—for the right price!

The "right price" is usually a choice cut of meat—either a ham or a beef roast; or sometimes a goat is offered—the plumper the better! The hopeful musician should stand at the top of the falls calling, "Fossegrim, oh

Old Erik Catches Hans, 1894
ARTIST: *H.J. Ford*

8

Fossegrim!" and toss the meat into the water. If he is quick, he might see a silvery arm shoot out from the curtain of water and snatch the meat. If the Fossegrim is in the right mood, and he likes the offering, he will grant the person the gift of music.

It is a painful process. At the next full moon the Fossegrim will leave his waterfall and visit the home of the human. Casting an enchantment over the sleeper, he bends and twists and tugs on his fingers until they crackle and pop and nearly break. In the morning the new musician will feel a dull ache, and after a day or so his fingers will be flexible and supple enough to play even the fastest notes.

Not all trolls are as talented or as smart as the Fossegrim, however. Most can be quite stupid and are easily tricked by clever humans. Yet there is one that can prove to be a match for anyone. That is Old Erik.

During the early days of Christianity, some monks came over from England to convert the Vikings. They knew that the Viking warriors feared almost nothing—not even their own gods. The monks knew that they could not change the people with good deeds and nice stories, so they told colorful stories of the harrows of hell, and brought with them the legend of a sinister and evil being, the Devil.

But the Vikings loved these tales! They renamed the Devil *Old Erik*, dressed him up as a tax collector, and sent him out to gather souls. He has horns and a beard like a goat, as well as one human foot and one cloven hoof. Many is the tale told of humans outwitting Old Erik, but many more are the legends in which Old Erik gets what he is after. Some story-tellers say that this devilish creature is closely related to the trolls, and perhaps may be master of them all.

Others say that it is the Dovre-Gubbe who is the Troll King. Far in the west of Norway there is a tall mountain known as the Dovre. It is beneath this rock that the King of the Trolls has his golden throne. He is sur-rounded by hundreds of other trolls, some as big as mountains themselves, others so small you have to squint to see them. The Dovre-Gubbe sits sulking on his throne, planning ways of ridding Norway of the pesky, meddling humans. Every once in a while some lost and wandering soul will stumble across Dovre-Gubbe's caverns and will never be heard from again.

Are all trolls hideously ugly? No.

There are some trolls who are more jealous of humans than malicious. They formed their own world beneath the Norwegian forests, an exact copy of the human world with farms, houses, and streets. They are of human size, kind of homely themselves, but they have attractive daughters who are sometimes called Haugtusser (Maids of the Mound) but are more often known as Huldrer.

Huldre women are incredibly beautiful, with long shining hair, rosy cheeks, and a bewitching smile. They do have one flaw, and that is a cow-like tail that they always try to keep hidden. Naive and innocent farm boys will often run across a Huldre in the forest or meadows, singing as beautifully as any siren. Sometimes the Huldre will spirit the young man to her underground world, where he must live with her forever, and sometimes she will fall in love with the human before she realizes what is happening to her. When this happens, she will agree to marry the young man in a Christian church. As soon as she does this, her tail will fall off, and she will become the best wife a man can ever hope for. Their children will often be more talented than most, and gifted with the second sight.

If a Huldre woman does not marry a mortal, she can live for three or four hundred years. As she grows older, she changes in appearance and becomes a Trollkjærring, a Troll Hag with a taste for human flesh. Sometimes she'll walk around the forest while carrying her head under her arm. Why does she do that? No one knows.

Foolish people often ask, "Do trolls still exist?"

These ancient stories can be told on many levels. Some say they are only stories; but the Old World Trolls are creatures of the night, caricatures of all that is evil in mankind. The legends warn children to be careful of the hidden dangers of the world and to mind their own manners. Each troll may be seen as a personification of a destructive and undesirable human trait or emotion. The stories are designed for self-reflection, to take notice of and correct the hidden "troll qualities" within ourselves. The troll does still exist, he exists in each one of us, and we must watch out for him.

A nice theory, really. But I wouldn't go walking alone in the dark Norwegian forests at night. . . .

—Joanne Asala

Farmer Weatherbeard, 1886
ARTIST: *Theodor Kittelsen*

Asbjørnsen and Moe

Saviors of the Trolls

For 800 years, since the coming of Christianity to Norway, the old gods and the trolls had been dying a slow death in the minds of the people. In its attempt to wipe out pagan beliefs, the church—particularly the pious and conservative Lutheran church—also attempted to rid its flock of old superstitions, legends and folktales. The Industrial Revolution left a further impact as families moved to the cities to work in factories; the long evenings sitting around the fire telling stories to one another were becoming a thing of the past. The trolls might have disappeared altogether if it were not for the rescue of the written word.

Norwegian folktales were first written down in the mid-1800s. Inspired by what the Brothers Grimm had done in the field of Germanic fairy tales, two students—Peter Christian Asbjørnsen and Jørgen Engebretsen Moe—decided to prepare a similar volume of the folktales and legends of their native land. In a letter to Jacob Grimm they wrote, "An early acquaintanceship with your *Kinder und Hausmärchen*, as well as an intimate knowledge of the life and lore of the people of Norway, gave us the idea to prepare a collection of Norwegian folktales."

But how should they be written? Asbjørnsen and Moe felt that the ornate style of the Grimms' tales would not do, and the current Norwegian literary style was also too formal, too "Danish." They decided that the stories should be written in a popular style, one which would stay as close as possible to the language, humor, vitality and colloquialisms of the tales as they were told in the mountains and vast forests of Norway. For the first time, Norwegian common speech appeared in print, and the stories reflected the strong imagination, independence and self-reliance of the peasant class.

The first volume of their tales, *Norske Folkeeventyr*, appeared in 1845, with a second edition in 1852. The tales became enormously popular and were translated into many languages. As a result, Asbjørnsen and Moe continued their research and traveled throughout the various districts of Norway gathering and retelling the folktales they encountered. Both showed a dedication unmatched in the field of folklore, although they had to make time for other careers to earn a living. Asbjørnsen became a zoologist and a forest inspector and Moe a clergyman who eventually became the bishop of Kristiansund—and a poet.

The two friends published additional volumes of their work, and many of the stories appeared in newspapers and magazines. When Moe's ever-increasing clerical duties took him away from active work in the field of folklore, his son, Moltke, continued the work of his father, eventually becoming a well-respected folklorist in his own right.

The early 1800s saw a period of romanticism in Norway, with a renewed interest in dance, costume, art and folklore. The publication of *Norske Folkeeventyr* had a huge impact on the Norwegian people; just as the *Kalevala* helped shape the independent spirit of the Finnish, so too did the folktales of Asbjørnsen and Moe help the Norwegians realize that even during the days of Danish dominance, the peasant class was able to maintain its own legends and beliefs. Asbjørnsen and Moe were able to present the world with a set of stories that was truly Norwegian. If these two friends had not hiked through the back-country, listening to and recording these legends, a rich body of troll stories might have been lost forever.

The Giant and the Giantess Who Tried to See
Who Could Count Fastest, 1907
ARTIST: *Theodor Kittelsen*

Werenskiold and Kittelsen

Nineteenth-Century Troll Artists

Asbjørnsen and Moe may have rescued the old troll stories and legends from oblivion, but it took illustrators like Erik Werenskiold and Theodor Kittelsen to give form to the dark imaginations of the people. From their brushes trolls would, for the first time, take shape and leer evilly from the pages of books.

For a long time Peter C. Asbjørnsen had wanted to do an illustrated version of the folktales, but it was not until 1877 that the project was under way. Some of the most famous Norwegian artists were selected to do the drawings, along with a young, relatively unknown man, Erik Werenskiold.

Werenskiold was born in Kongsvinger, where he grew up listening to his father read from the ancient Norse myths and sagas. Asbjørnsen saw several of Werenskiold's sketches and asked him to participate in the project. The first picture Werenskiold did was for the tale *Taper Tom Who Made the King's Daughter Laugh*. Werenskiold, who had been studying and working in the artists' mecca of München, realized that he had seen very little of Norway and went to Lom and Vågå to familiarize himself with the setting of the tales. In the farms and villages of the back country, he found that the old patriarchal customs and traditions were still alive. He wrote, "Here on the great farms there are still small kings, and the tenant farmers are their serfs. Behind this primitive life, behind these vigorous, strongly pronounced human types, and this unique architecture, one could sense the Middle Ages; and behind the large forest lay the Troll World of the Jotunheim Mountains. I have never seen anything more Norwegian to me than Vågå."

The illustrations established Werenskiold as one of the foremost artists of Norway. Of the original group of artists, he alone was asked to do the drawings for a second edition. But Werenskiold, who had a number of other tempting offers, immediately suggested a friend of his for the job, an unknown artist named Theodor Kittelsen. "Kittelsen has a wild, individual, inventive fantasy," he wrote. "For many years I have had the constant thought that he should be the man to do that side of your *eventyr* which none of us has yet been able to accomplish, namely the purely, fantastic creations!"

When Asbjørnsen saw the first illustrations submitted by Kittelsen, he was shocked. He thought that the pictures for *The Ash Lad Who Had an Eating Match with the Troll, Buttercup,* and *The Golden Bird* were of a superior quality, but that the trolls, with their wildly grotesque, repellent and ugly features, were too terrifying for young children. But after it was proved that children were not frightened to death and actually craved such illustrations, *A Book of Fairytales for Children* appeared with a dozen of Kittelsen's drawings, placing him side by side with Werenskiold as a premiere troll illustrator.

Biographer Leif Østby, in his book *Theodor Kittelsen,* said of Kittelsen's trolls, "They rarely possess the good-natured stupidity of Werenskiold's creations, they exude an air of the horrific and weird. Even when they laugh, they often provoke shudders of fear." Kittelsen's own son, Helge, wrote about his childhood memories, "We never got to see a troll up close, but we knew they were never far away—especially when we walked alone. We preferred to be with Papa if we should ever meet a troll, for then we didn't need to be frightened. We knew for sure that Papa had met the troll, the Nøkk and the Huldre nymph, and we thought it quite natural when he said of another illustrator, 'He is going to sketch trolls? Him? He has never seen a troll in his life!' We children felt insulted if anyone later tried to draw trolls, for they had no idea what trolls looked like."

Kittelsen, perhaps for the first time, was able to create fantastic creatures that sprang directly from the natural background, from the forests, lakes and bleak mountainsides of Norway. A tree-covered ridge, a large boulder or an overturned tree stump might appear, at second glance, to be the head of a troll. Kittelsen himself wrote, "These are the same faces as those that grew, in the eyes of our ancestors, into a world of giants and trolls." In 1892 he produced both pictures and text for a book of his own called *Troll Magic.*

The tales of Asbjørnsen, Moe, and Kittelsen, illustrated by Werenskiold and Kittelsen, soon became national treasures. Without a doubt these legends have had an impact on and have become a permanent part of Norway's literary history, and they may still be read with the same enthusiasm and enjoyment as when they were first published.

Self-portrait with Admiring Animals, 1887
ARTIST: *Theodor Kittelsen*

Buttercup

by Peter Christian Asbjørnsen
translated by George Webbe Dasent

Once on a time there was an old wife who was fond of baking. Now you must know that this old wife had a little son who was so plump and fat, and so fond of good things, that they called him Buttercup. She had a dog,

Buttercup, 1882-3
ARTIST: *Theodor Kittelsen*

too, whose name was Goldtooth, and as she was baking one day, Goldtooth began to bark.

"Run out, Buttercup, there's a deer!" said the old wife. "See what Goldtooth is barking at."

So the boy ran out, and came back crying, "Oh, Heaven help me! Here comes a great big troll witch, with her head under her arm, and a bag at her back!"

"Jump under the bread board and hide yourself," said his mother.

In came the old hag.

"Good day," she said.

"God bless you!" said Buttercup's mother.

"Isn't your Buttercup at home today?" asked the hag.

"No, no he isn't. He's out in the wood with his father shooting ptarmigan."

"Plague take it all," said the hag, "for I had such a nice little silver knife I wanted to give him."

"Pip, pip! Here I am!" said Buttercup under the bread board, and out he came.

"I'm so old and stiff in the back," said the hag, "you must creep into the bag and fetch it out for yourself."

But when Buttercup was well into the bag, the troll hag threw it over her back and strode off, and when they had gone a good bit of the way, the old hag got tired and asked, "How far is it off to Snoring?"

"Half a mile," answered Buttercup.

So the hag put down her sack on the road, and went aside by herself into the wood, and lay down to sleep. Meantime Buttercup set to work and cut a hole in the sack with his knife; then he crept out and put a great root of a firtree into the sack, and ran home to his mother.

When the hag got home and saw what there was in the sack, you may fancy she was in a fine rage.

Next day the old wife sat and baked again, and her dog began to bark, just as he did the day before.

"Run out, Buttercup, my boy," she said, "and see what Goldtooth is barking at."

"Well, I never!" cried Buttercup as soon as he got out. "If there isn't that ugly old beast coming again with her head under her arm, and a great sack at her back."

"Under the bread board with you and hide," said his mother.

"Good day!" said the hag. "Is your Buttercup at home?"

"No. I'm sorry to say that he isn't," said his mother. "He's out in the forest with his father chopping wood."

"What a bore," said the hag. "Here I have a beautiful little silver spoon I want to give him."

"Pip, pip! Here I am!" said Buttercup, and crept out.

"I'm so stiff in the back," said the old troll witch, "you must creep into the sack and fetch it out yourself."

So when Buttercup was well into the sack, the troll hag swung it over her shoulders and set off home as fast as her legs could carry her. But when they had gone a good bit, she grew weary and asked, "How far is it off to Snoring?"

"About a mile and a half," answered Buttercup from the bag.

So the hag set down the sack and went aside into the wood to sleep a bit. But while she slept, Buttercup made a hole in the sack and got out, and put a great stone into it. Now, when the old witch got home, she made a great fire on the hearth, and put a big pot on it, and got everything ready to boil Buttercup; but when she took the sack, and thought she was going to turn out Buttercup into the pot, down plumped the stone and made a hole in the bottom of the pot, so that the water ran out and quenched the fire. Then the old hag was in a dreadful rage, and said, "No matter if he makes himself ever so heavy next time, I shall trick him again, I will!"

The third day everything went just as it had gone twice before; Goldtooth began to bark, and Buttercup's mother said to him, "Do run out and see what our dog is barking at."

From "Buttercup," 1882-3
ARTIST: *Theodor Kittelsen*

So out he went, but he soon came back crying out, "Heaven save us! Here comes the old hag again with her head under her arm, and a sack at her back."

"Quickly! Jump under the bread board and hide," said his mother.

"Good day!" said the hag as she came in at the door. "Is your Buttercup at home today?"

"You're very kind to ask after him," said his mother. "But he's out at the stream fishing with his father."

"What a bore now," said the old hag. "Here I have such a beautiful little silver fork for him."

"Pip, pip! Here I am!" said Buttercup as he came out from under the bread board.

"I'm so stiff in the back," said the hag, "you must creep into the sack and fetch it out for yourself."

But when Buttercup was well inside the sack, the old hag swung it across her shoulders, and set off as fast as she could. This time she did not turn aside to sleep by the way, but went straight home with Buttercup in the sack. When she reached her house it was Sunday.

So the troll hag said to her daughter, "Now you must take Buttercup and kill him, and boil him nicely till I come back, for I'm off to church to invite my guests to dinner."

So, when all in the house were gone to church, the daughter was to take Buttercup and kill him; but then she didn't know how to set about it at all.

"Stop a bit," said Buttercup. "I'll soon show you how to do it; just lay your head on the chopping block, and you'll soon see."

So the poor silly thing laid her head down, and Buttercup took an axe and chopped her head off, just as if she had been a chicken. Then he laid her head in the bed, and popped her body into the pot, and boiled it so nicely; and when he had done that, he climbed up on the roof, and dragged up with him the firtree root and the stone, and put the one over the door, and the other at the top of the chimney.

So when the household came back from church, and saw the head on the bed, they thought it was the daughter who lay there asleep; and then they thought they would just taste the broth.

"Good, by my troth! Buttercup broth," said the old hag.

"Good, by my troth! Daughter broth," said Buttercup down the chimney, but no one heeded him.

So the old hag's husband, who was every bit as bad as she, took the spoon to have a taste.

From "Buttercup," 1882-3
ARTIST: *Theodor Kittelsen*

"Good, by my troth! Buttercup broth," said he.

"Good, by my troth! Daughter broth," said Buttercup down the chimney pipe.

Then they all began to wonder who it could be that chattered on so, and ran out to see; but when they came out at the door, Buttercup threw down on them the firtree root and the stone, and broke all their heads to bits. After that he took all the gold and silver that lay in the house, and went home to his mother, and became a rich man.

From "Prince Ring," retold by Andrew Lang, 1894
ARTIST: *H. J. Ford*

Henry J. Ford—not to be confused with the Henry Ford of automobile history—was a popular illustrator of the late 19th century. He is perhaps best known for the exquisite black-and-white illustrations which accompany Andrew Lang's famous fairy books. Ford's art has a certain pre-Raphaelite style, and his attention to detail sets him apart from all others. Born in London, he studied at the Slade and at Hubert von Herkomer's Bushey School of Art. In addition to his work in children's literature, Ford's illustrations appeared in many adult books and magazines of the day.

The Trolls in Hedale Wood, 1878
ARTIST: *Erik Werenskiold*

The Trolls in Hedale Wood

by Peter Christian Asbjørnsen
translated by George Webbe Dasent

Up at a place in Vaage, in Gudbrandsdalen, there lived in the olden days a very poor couple. They had many children, and two of the sons, who were about half-grown up, were forced to roam about the countryside, begging. So it was that they were well acquainted with all the highways and by-ways, and they knew the shortcut into Hedale.

It happened once that they wanted to go there, but at the same time they heard that some falconers had built themselves a hut at Maela. They wished to kill two birds with one stone, and see the falcons, and how they are taken, and so they took the short cut across to Hedale.

But you must know it was far on towards autumn, and so the milk-maids had all gone home from the shielings, and they could neither get shelter nor food. Then they had to keep straight on for Hedale, but the path was a mere track, and when night fell they lost it. Worse still, they could not find the falconers' hut either. Before they knew where they were, they found themselves in the very depths of the forest. As soon as they saw that they could not go on, they began to break boughs, lit a fire, and built themselves a bower of branches, for they had a hand-axe with them. Then they plucked soft heather and moss and made themselves a bed.

A little while after they had lain down, they heard something which sniffed and snuffed so with its nose. The boys pricked up their ears and listened sharp to hear whether it was wild beasts or Wood Trolls, and just then something snuffled up the air louder than ever and said, "There's a smell of Christian blood here!"

At the same time they heard such a heavy footfall that the Earth shook under it, and then they knew well enough the trolls must be about.

"Heaven help us! Heaven help us! What shall we do?" said the younger boy to his brother.

"You must stand as you are under the fir-tree, and be ready to take our bags and run away when you see them coming; as for myself, I'll take the axe."

All at once they saw the trolls coming at them, and they were so tall, their heads were just as high as the fir-tops. They had only one eye between all three, and they took turns using it. Each had a hole in his forehead into which he put it, and turned and twisted it with his hands. The one in front had to have it to see his way, and the others went behind, holding on to the one ahead.

"Take up the traps," said the elder of the boys, "but don't run away too far. Stay and see how things go. As they carry their eye so high aloft, they'll find it hard to see me when I get behind them."

"Okay," said the younger brother, and he ran off, the trolls after him. Meanwhile the elder got behind them and chopped the hindmost troll with his axe on the ankle, so that the troll gave an awful shriek, and the foremost troll got so afraid he was all of a shake and dropped the eye. But the boy was not slow to snap it up. It was bigger than two quart pots put together, and so clear and bright, that though it was pitch dark, everything was as clear as day as soon as he looked through it.

When the trolls realized that he had taken their eye and done one of them harm, they began to threaten him with all the evil in the world if he didn't give back the eye at once.

"I don't care a farthing for trolls and threats," said the boy. "Now I've got three eyes to myself and you three have got none. And besides, two of you now have to carry the third."

"If we don't get our eye back this minute, you shall both be turned to sticks and stones!" screeched the trolls.

But the boy thought things needn't go so fast; he was not afraid of witchcraft or hard words. "If you don't leave me in peace, I'll chop all three of you so that you will have to creep and crawl along the earth like insects and crabs."

When the trolls heard that, they got still more afraid and began to use soft words. They begged so prettily that he give them back their eye. "You shall have both gold and silver and all that you wish!"

That seemed very fine to the lad, so he said that if one of them would go home and fetch as much gold and silver as would fill their bags, and give each of them a good crossbow besides, that they might have their eye back. "But I will keep it until you do as I say."

The trolls were very cross and put out, and said that none of them would go when he hadn't his eye to see with. But then one of them began to bawl out for their wife, for you must know that they had one wife between them all as well as one eye. After awhile an answer came from a knoll a long way off to the north. The trolls said that she must come with two steel crossbows and two buckets full of gold and silver; and then it was not long, you may fancy, before she was there.

When she heard what had happened, she too began to threaten them with witchcraft. But the trolls by now were so afraid, and begged her beware of the little wasp, for she couldn't be sure he would not take away her eye, too.

So she threw them the crossbows and the buckets and the gold and silver, and strode off to the knoll with the trolls; and since that time no one has ever heard that the trolls have walked in Hedale Wood sniffing out Christian blood.

The Boys Return Home
ARTIST: *Erik Werenskiold*

From "The Golden Bird," 1883
ARTIST: *Theodor Kittelsen*

The Golden Bird

by Peter Christian Asbjørnsen
translated by George Webbe Dasent

Once on a time there was a king who had a garden, and in that garden stood an apple tree, and on that apple tree grew one golden apple every year. But when the time drew near for plucking it, away it went, and there was no one who could tell who took it or what became of it. It was gone, and that was all they knew.

This king had three sons. So one day he told them that the one who could get him his apple again, or lay hold of the thief who had stolen it, should inherit the kingdom after him, no matter if he were the eldest, or the youngest, or the midmost.

The eldest set out first on this quest and sat down under the tree to watch for the thief. When night drew near, a golden bird came flying by, and his feathers gleamed from a long way off. But when the king's son saw the bird and the light, he got so afraid he dared not stay his watch, but ran back into the palace as fast as ever he could.

The next morning the apple was gone. By that time the king's son had got back his heart into his body, and so he fell to filling his scrip with food, and was all for setting out to try if he could find the bird. So the king fitted him out well, and spared neither money nor clothes.

When the king's son had gone a bit, he got hungry and took out his scrip, and sat down to eat his dinner by the wayside. Just then a fox came out from a spruce clump and sat down and looked at him.

"Do, dear friend, give me a morsel of food," said the fox.

"I'll give you burnt horn, that I will," said the king's son. "I'm likely to need food myself, for no one knows how far and how long I may have to travel."

"Oh! So that's your game, is it?" said the fox, and disappeared back into the wood.

When the king's son had eaten and rested awhile, he set off on his way again. After a long, long time he came to a great town, and in that town was an inn where there was always mirth and never sorrow. There he thought it would be good to be, and so he turned in there. There was so much dancing and drinking, and fun and jollity, that he forgot the bird and its feathers, and his father and his quest; in fact he forgot the whole kingdom. Away he was and away he stayed.

The year after, the king's midmost son was to watch for the apple thief in the garden. Yes, he too sat down under the tree when it began to ripen. So all at once one night the golden bird came shining like the sun, and the lad got so afraid he put his tail between his legs and ran indoors as fast as ever he could.

The next morning the apple was gone, but by that time the king's son had taken heart again, and was all for setting off to see if he could find the bird. Yes, he began to put up his traveling fare, and the king fitted him out well, and spared neither clothes nor money. But just the same befell him as had befallen his brother. When he had traveled a bit he got hungry, and opened his scrip, and sat down to eat his dinner by the wayside. Out came a fox from a spruce clump and sat down and looked on.

"Dear friend, give me a morsel, do?" said the fox.

"I'll give you burnt horn, that I will," said the king's son. "I may come to need food myself, for no one knows how far and how long I may have to go."

"Oh, so that's your game, is it?" said the fox, and away he went into the wood again.

When the king's son had eaten and rested himself awhile, he set off on his way again. And after a long time he came to the same town and the same inn where there was always mirth and never sorrow, and he too thought it would be good to turn in there.

The very first man he met was his brother, and so he too stayed there. His brother had feasted and drunk till he had scarce any clothes on his back. But now they both began anew, and there was such drinking and dancing and fun and jollity, that the second brother also forgot the bird and its feathers, and his father, the quest, and the whole kingdom. Away he was and away he stayed.

When the time drew on that the apple was getting ripe again, the king's youngest son was to go out into the garden and watch for the apple thief. Now he took with him a comrade who was to help him up into the tree, and they took with them a keg of ale and a pack of cards to while away the time so that they should not fall asleep.

All at once came a blaze as of the sun, and just as the golden bird pounced down and snapped up the apple, the king's son tried to seize it, but he only got a feather out of its tail. When he got back to the castle, he went into the king's bedroom. When he brought in the feather the room was as bright as broad day.

He too decided he would go out into the wide world to try, if he could, to hear any tidings of his brothers and catch the golden bird. After all, he had been so near it that he had put his mark on it and got a feather out of its tail. The king was long in making up his mind if he should let him go, for he thought it would not be better with him who was the youngest than with the eldest, who ought to have had more knowledge of the ways of the world. He was afraid that he might lose him, too. But the king's son begged so prettily that he had to give him leave at last.

So the youngest son began to pack up his traveling fare, and the king fitted him out well both with clothes and money, and so he set off. When he had traveled a bit he got hungry and opened his scrip, and sat down to eat his dinner, and just as he put the first bite into his mouth, a fox came out of a spruce clump and sat down by him and looked on.

"Oh, dear friend! Please give me a morsel of food, do!" said the fox.

"I might very well come to need food for myself," said the king's son, "for, I'm sure, I can't tell how long I shall have to go; but so much I know, that I can just give you a little bit."

So when the fox had got a bit of meat to bite at, he asked the king's son whither he was bound. Well, he told him what he was trying to do.

"If you will listen to me," said the fox, "I will help you, so that you shall take luck along with you."

Then the king's son gave his word to listen to him, and so they set off in company, and when they had traveled awhile they came to the selfsame town and the selfsame inn where there was always mirth and never sorrow.

"Now I may just as well stay outside the town," said the fox. "Those dogs are such a bore." And then the fox told him what his brothers had done, and what they were still doing, and he went on. "If you go in there you'll get no farther either. Do you hear?"

So the king's son gave his word and his hand into the bargain that he wouldn't go in there, and each went his way. But when the prince got to the inn and heard what music and jollity there was inside, he could not help going in. There were not two words about that, and when he met his brothers, there was such a to-do that he forgot both the fox and his quest, and the bird and his father. But when he had been there awhile the fox came—for he had ventured into the town after all—and peeped through the door, and winked at the king's son, and said now they must set off. So the prince came to his senses again, and away they started for the house.

And when they had gone awhile they saw a big fell far, far off. Then the fox said, "Three-hundred miles behind yon fell there grows a gilded linden tree with golden leaves, and in that linden roosts the golden bird whose feather that is."

So they traveled together, and when the king's son was going off to catch the bird, the fox gave him some fine feathers, which he was to wave with his hand to lure the bird down, and then it would come flying and perch on his hand. But the fox told him to find and not touch the linden, for there was a big troll who owned it, and if the king's son but touched the tiniest twig the troll would come and slay him on the spot.

The king's son assured him that he would not touch it, but when he had got the bird on his fist, he thought he would just have a twig of the linden, that was past praying against, it was so bright and lovely. So he took just one, just one very tiny little one. But in a trice out came the troll.

"WHO IS IT THAT STEALS MY LINDEN AND MY BIRD?" he roared, and was so angry that sparks of fire flashed from him.

"Thieves think every man a thief," said the king's son, "but none are hanged but those who don't steal right."

But the troll said it was all one, and was just going to smite him, but the lad said that he must spare his life.

"Well, well!" said the troll. "If you can get for me again the horse which my nearest neighbor has stolen from me, you shall get off with your life."

"But where shall I find him?" asked the king's son.

"Oh, he lives three-hundred miles beyond yon big fell that looks blue in the sky."

So the king's son gave his word to do his best. But when he met the fox, Reynard was not altogether in a soft temper. "Now you have behaved badly," he said. "Had you done as I bade you, we should have been on our way home by this time."

So they had to make a fresh start, as life was at stake, and the prince had given his word, and after a long, long time they got to the spot. And when the prince was to go and take the horse, the fox said, "When you come into the stable, you will see many bits hanging on the stalls, both of silver and gold; those you shall not touch, for then the troll will come out and slay you on the spot, but the ugliest and poorest, that you shall take."

The king's son gave his word to do that, but when he got into the stable he thought it was all stuff, for there was enough and to spare of fine bits; and so he took the brightest he could find, and it shone like gold; but in a trice out came the troll, so cross that sparks of fire flashed from him.

"WHO IS IT WHO TRIES TO STEAL MY HORSE AND MY BIT?" he roared out.

"Thieves think every man a thief," said the king's son, "but none are hanged but those who don't steal right."

"Well, all the same," said the troll, "I'll kill you on the spot."

But the king's son said he must spare his life.

"Well, well!" said the troll. "If you can get me back the lovely maiden my nearest neighbor has stolen from me, I'll spare your life."

"Where does he live, then?" asked the king's son.

"Oh, he lives three-hundred miles behind that big fell that is blue, yonder in the sky," said the troll.

The king's son gave his word to fetch the maiden, and then he had leave to go, and got off with his life. But when he came out-of-doors, the fox was not in the very best temper, you may fancy.

"Now you have behaved badly again. Had you done as I bade you, we might have been on our way home long ago. Do you know, I almost think now I won't stay with you a moment longer."

But the king's son begged and prayed so prettily from the bottom of his heart, and gave his word never to do anything but what the fox said, if he would only be his companion. At last the fox yielded, and they became fast friends again, and so they set off afresh, and after a long, long time they came to the spot where the lovely maiden was.

"Yes," said the fox, "you have given your word like a man, but for all that, I dare not let you go into the troll's house this time. I must go myself."

So he went in, and in a little while he came out with the maiden, and so they traveled back by the same way that they had come. And when they came back to the troll who had the horse, they took both it and the grandest bit, and when they got to the troll who owned the linden and the golden bird, they took both the linden and the bird, and set off with them.

When they had traveled awhile, they came to a field of rye, and the fox said, "I hear a noise, now you must ride on alone, and I will bide here awhile."

The fox platted himself a dress of rye-straw, and it looked just like someone who stood there and preached. And he had scarcely done that before all three trolls came flying along, thinking they would overtake the thieves.

"Have you seen anyone riding by here with a lovely maiden, and a horse with a gold bit, and a golden bird and a gilded linden tree?" they all roared out to him who stood there preaching.

"Yes! I heard that from my grandmother's grandmother, that such a train passed by here. But, Lord bless us, that was in the good old time when my grandmother's grandmother baked cakes for a penny and gave the penny back again."

Then all the three trolls burst out into fits of laughter, "HA! HA! HA! HA!" they cried, and took hold of one another.

"If we have slept so long, we may e'en just turn our noses home, and go to bed," they said, and so they went back the way they had come.

Then the fox started off after the king's son, but when they got to the town where the inn and his brothers were, he said, "I dare not go through the town for fear of the dogs. I must take my own way round about, and you must take good care that your brothers don't lay hold of you."

When the king's son got into town, he thought it very hard if he didn't look in on his brothers and have a word with them, and so he halted a little time. But as soon as his brothers set eyes on him, they came out and took from him both the maiden and the horse, the bird and the linden, and everything; and himself they stuffed into a cask and cast him into the lake. And so they set off home to the king's palace, with the maiden and the horse, and the bird and the linden, and everything. But the maiden wouldn't say a word; she got pale and wretched to look at. The horse got so thin and starved, all his bones scarce clung together. The bird moped and shone no more, and the linden withered away.

Meanwhile, the fox walked about outside the town, where the inn was with all its jollity, and he listened and waited for the king's son and the lovely maiden, and wondered why they did not come back. So he went hither and thither, and waited and longed, and at last he went down to the strand, and there he saw the cask which lay on the lake drifting, and called out:

"Are you driven about there, you empty cask?"

"Oh! It is I, the king's son!" said a muffled voice from within the cask.

Then the fox swam out into the lake as fast as he could, and got hold of the cask and drew it on shore. Then he began to gnaw at the hoops, and when he had got them off the cask, he called out, "Kick and stamp!"

So the king's son struck out and stamped and kicked, till every stave burst asunder, and out he jumped from the cask. Then they went together to the king's palace, and when they got there the maiden grew lovely, and began to speak; the horse got so fat and sleek that every hair beamed; the bird shone and sang; the linden began to bloom and glitter with its leaves, and at last the maiden said, "Here he is who set us free!"

They planted the linden in the garden and the youngest prince was to have the princess (for, you must know, she was indeed a princess), but as for the two elder brothers, they put them each into his own cask, full of nails, and rolled them down a steep hill.

So they made ready for the bridal; but first the fox said to the prince that he must lay him on the chopping block, and cut his head off, and whether he thought it good or ill, there was no help for it, he must do it. But as the prince dealt the stroke, the fox became a handsome prince, and he was the princess's brother, whom they had set free from the trolls.

So the bridal day came on, and it was so great and grand that the story of that feasting spread far and wide, till it reached all the way to this very spot.

The Companion

by Peter Christian Asbjørnsen
translated by George Webbe Dasent

Once on a time there was a farmer's son who dreamt that he was to marry a princess far, far out in the world. She was as red and white as milk and blood, and so rich there was no end to her riches. When he awoke he seemed to see her still standing bright and living before him, and he thought her so sweet and lovely that his life was not worth having unless he had her, too. So he sold all he had, and set off into the world to find her. Well, he went far, and farther than far, and about winter he came to a land where all the high roads lay right straight on end; there wasn't a bend in any of them. When he had wandered on and on for a quarter of a year, he came to a town, and outside the church door lay a big block of ice in which there stood a dead body, and the whole parish spat on it as they passed by to the church. The lad wondered at this, and when the priest came out of church he asked him what it all meant.

"It is a great wrong-doer," said the priest. "He has been executed for his ungodliness, and set up there to be mocked and spat upon."

"But what was his wrong-doing?" asked the lad.

"When he was alive, he was a vintner," said the priest, "and he mixed water with his wine."

The lad thought that this was not a dreadful sin, and said, "Well, after he had atoned for it with his life, you might as well have let him have Christian burial and peace after death."

But the priest said that could not in any way be, for there must be folk to break him out of the ice, and money to buy a grave from the church; then the grave digger must be paid for digging the grave, and the sexton for tolling the bell, and the clerk for singing the hymns, and the priest for sprinkling dust over him. "Do you think now there would be anyone who would be willing to pay all this for an executed sinner?"

"Yes," said the lad. "If I could only get him buried in Christian earth, I would be sure to pay for his funeral ale out of my scanty means."

Even with these words the priest hemmed and hawed, but when the lad came with two witnesses, and asked him in their hearing if he could refuse to sprinkle dust over the corpse, he was forced to answer that he could not.

So they broke the vintner out of the block of ice, and laid him in Christian earth, and they tolled the bell and sang hymns over him, and the priest sprinkled dust over him, and they drank his funeral ale till they wept and laughed by turns; but when the lad had paid for the ale, he hadn't many pence left in his pocket.

He set off on his way again, but he hadn't got far before a man overtook him who asked if he did not think it dull work walking on alone.

"No," said the lad, "I do not think it dull. I have always something to think about."

Then the man asked if he wouldn't like to have a servant.

"No," said the lad. "I am wont to be my own servant. Therefore I have need of none, and even if I wanted one ever so much, I have no means to get one, for I have no money to pay for his food and wages."

"You do not need a servant, that I know better than you," said the man. "But you have need of one whom you can trust in life and death. If you won't have me as a servant, you may take me as a companion; I give you my word I will stand you in good stead, and it shan't cost you a penny. I will pay my own fare, and as for food and clothing, you shall have no trouble about them."

Well, on those terms the lad was willing enough to have him as a companion, so after that they traveled together, and the man, for the most part, went on ahead and showed the lad the way.

So after they had traveled on and on from land to land, over hill and wood, they came to a crossfell that stopped the way. There the companion went up and knocked, and bade them open the door, and the rock opened sure enough, and when they got inside the hill, up came an old troll witch with a chair, and asked them, "Be so good as to sit down. No doubt you are weary."

"Sit on it yourself," said the man. So she was forced to take her seat, and as soon as she sat down she stuck fast, for the chair was such that it let no one loose that came near it. Meanwhile, they went about inside the hill, and the companion looked 'round till he saw a sword hanging over the door. That he would have, and he gave his word to the troll witch that if he got it he would let her loose out of the chair.

"No!" she screeched out. "Ask me anything else. Anything else you may have, surely, but not that, for it is my *Three-Sister Sword*. We are three sisters who own it together."

"Very well, then you may sit there till the end of the world," said the companion. But when she heard that, the troll witch said he might have it if he would set her free.

So he took the sword and went off with it, and left her still sitting there. When they had gone far, far away over the naked fells and wide wastes, they came to another crossfell. There, too, the companion knocked and bade them open the door, and the same thing happened as happened before. The rock opened, and when they had got a good way into the hill another old troll witch came up to them with a chair and begged them to sit down. "Ye may well be weary," she said.

"Sit down yourself," said the companion. And so she fared as her sister had fared. She did not dare to say nay, and as soon as she sat on the chair she stuck fast. Meanwhile the lad and his companion went about in the hill, and the man broke open all the chests and drawers till he found what he sought, and that was a golden ball of yarn. That he set his heart on, and he promised the troll witch that he would set her free if she would give him the golden ball. She said he might take all she had, but that she could not part with the ball of yarn. "It is my *Three-Sister Ball.*" But when she heard that she would sit there till doomsday unless he got it, she said he might take it if he would only set her free. So the companion took the golden ball, but he left her sitting where she sat.

From "The Companion," 1886
ARTIST: *Erik Werenskiold*

So on went the lad and the companion for many days, over waste and wood, till they came to a third crossfell. There all went as it had gone twice before. The companion knocked, the rock opened, and inside the hill an old troll witch came up, and asked them to sit on her chair, they must be so tired. The companion said again, "Sit on it yourself." And there she sat. They had not gone through many rooms before they saw an old hat which hung on a peg behind the door. That the companion must and would have! But the troll witch said she couldn't part with it. "It is my *Three-Sister Hat*, and if I gave it away, all my luck would be lost." But when she heard that she would have to sit there till the end of the world unless he got it, she said he might take it and let her loose. When the companion had got well hold of the hat, he went off, and bade her sit there still, like the rest of them.

After a long, long time the lad and his companion came to a Sound. Then the companion took the ball of yarn, and threw it so hard against the rock on the other side of the stream that it bounded back, and after he had thrown it backwards and forwards a few times it became a bridge. On that bridge they went over the Sound, and when they reached the other side, the man bade the lad to be quick and wind up the yarn as soon as he could, for, said he, "If we don't wind it up quick, all those troll witches will set themselves free and come after us, and tear us to bits."

So the lad wound and wound with all his might and main, and when there was no more to wind than the very last thread, up came the old troll witches on the wings of the wind. They flew to the water, so that the spray rose before them, and snatched at the end of the thread; but they could not quite get hold of it, and so they were drowned in the Sound.

When they had traveled a few days farther, the companion said, "Now we are coming to the castle where she is, the princess of whom you dreamt, and when we get there you must go in and tell the king what you are seeking."

When they reached the castle the lad did as the man told him, and was very heartily welcomed. He had a room for himself, and another for his friend, and when dinnertime drew near, he was bidden to dine at the king's own board. As soon as ever he set eyes on the princess, he knew her at once, and saw it was she of whom he had dreamt as his bride. Then he told her his business, and she answered that she liked him well enough, and would gladly have him; but first he must undergo three trials. When they had dined, she gave him a pair of golden scissors and said:

"The first proof is that you must take these scissors and keep them, and give them to me at mid-day tomorrow. It is not so very great a trial, I fancy," she said, and made a face, "but if you can't stand it, you lose your life. It is the law, and so you will be drawn and quartered, and your body will be stuck on stakes, and your head over the gate, just like those lovers of mine, whose skulls and skeletons you see outside the window."

"That is no such great art," thought the lad.

But the princess was so merry and mad, and flirted so much with him, that he forgot all about the scissors and himself, and so while they played and sported, she stole the scissors away from him without his knowing it. When he went up to his room that night, and told his companion how he had fared, and what she said to him, and about the scissors she gave him to keep, the companion said, "Of course you have the scissors safe and sure."

The lad searched in all his pockets, but there were no scissors, and he was in a sad way when he found them wanting.

"Well, well!" said the companion. "I'll see if I can't get you them again."

With that he went down into the stable, and there stood a big, fat billygoat which belonged to the princess, and it was of that breed that it could fly many times faster through the air than it could run on land. So the companion took the *Three-Sister Sword* and gave the billygoat a stroke between the horns and said, "When rides the princess to see her lover tonight?"

The billygoat baaed, and said it dared not say, but when it had another stroke, it said the princess was coming at eleven o'clock. Then the companion put on the *Three-Sister Hat*, and all at once he became invisible, and he waited for her. When she came in, she took and rubbed the billygoat with an ointment which she had in a great horn and said, "Away, away, o'er roof, tree, and steeple, o'er land, o'er sea, o'er hill, o'er dale, to my true love who awaits me this night in the fell."

At the very moment that the goat set off, the companion threw himself behind, and away they went like a blast through the air. They were not long on the way, and in a trice they came to a crossfell. There the princess knocked, and passed through the fell to the troll, who was her lover.

"Now, my dear," she said to him. "A new lover is come, whose heart is set on having me. He is young and handsome, but I will have no other than you." And so she coaxed and petted the troll. "I set him a trial, and here are the scissors he was to watch and keep. Now do you keep them."

The two laughed heartily together, just as though they had the lad already on wheel and stake.

"Yes, yes!" said the troll. "I'll keep them safe enough. *And I shall sleep in the bride's white arms, while ravens round his skeleton swarm.*"

So the troll laid the scissors in an iron chest with three locks, but just as he dropped them into the chest, the companion snapped them up. Neither the troll nor the princess could see him, for he still had on the *Three-Sister Hat*, and so the troll locked up the chest for naught, and he hid the key he had in the hollow eye-tooth in which he had the toothache. There it would be hard work for anyone to find it, the troll thought.

When midnight had passed, the princess set off home again. The companion got up behind the goat, and they lost no time on the way back.

Next day, about noon, the lad was asked down to the board, but then the princess gave herself such airs, and was so high and mighty, she would scarce look towards the side where the lad sat. After they had dined, she dressed her face in holiday garb, and said, as if butter wouldn't melt in her mouth, "Maybe you have those scissors which I begged you to keep yesterday?"

"Oh, yes, I have," said the lad, "and here they are."

With those words he pulled them out, and drove them into the board, till it jumped back again.

The princess could not have been more vexed had he driven the scissors into her face, but for all that, she made herself soft and gentle and said, "Since you have kept the scissors so well, it won't be any trouble to you to keep my golden ball of yarn. Take care you give it to me tomorrow at noon, but if you have lost it, you shall lose your life on the scaffold. It is the law."

The lad thought that an easy thing, so he took and put the golden ball into his pocket. But she fell a-playing and flirting with him again, so that he forgot both himself and the golden ball, and while they were at the height of their games and pranks, she stole it from him, and sent him off to bed.

When the lad came up to his bedroom, and told what they had said and done, his companion asked, "Of course you have the golden ball she gave you?"

"Yes, yes!" said the lad, and felt in his pocket where he had put it. But no! There was no ball to be found, and he fell again into such an ill mood, and knew not which way to turn.

"Well, well, bear up a bit," said the companion. "I'll see if I can't lay hands on it," and with that he took the sword and hat and strode off to a smith, and got twelve pounds of iron welded on the back of the sword-blade. Then he went down to the stable, and gave the billygoat a stroke between his horns, so that the brute went head over heels, and he asked, "When rides the princess to see her lover tonight?"

"At twelve o'clock," baaed the billygoat, shaking his head. The companion put on the *Three-Sister Hat* again, and waited till she came, tearing along with her horn of ointment, and greased the billygoat. Then she said, as she had said the first time, "Away, away, o'er roof, tree, and steeple, o'er land, o'er sea, o'er hill, o'er dale, to my true love who awaits me this night in the fell."

In a trice they were off, and the companion threw himself on behind the billygoat, and away they went like a blast through the air. In the twinkling of an eye they came to the troll's hill, and when she had knocked three times, they passed through the rock to the troll, who was her lover.

"Where was it you hid the golden scissors I gave you yesterday, my darling?" cried out the princess. "My wooer had it and gave it back to me."

"That is quite impossible," said the troll, "for I locked it up in a chest with three locks and hid the keys in the hollow of my eye-tooth." But when they unlocked the chest, and looked for it, the troll had no scissors in his chest.

So the princess told him how she had given her suitor her golden ball. "And here it is!" she beamed. "I took it from him again without his knowing it. But what shall we hit upon now, since he is a master of such craft!"

Well, the troll hardly knew, but after they had thought a bit, they made up their minds to light a large fire and burn the golden ball so they would be cocksure that he could not get at it. But, just as the princess tossed it into the fire, the companion stood ready and caught it. Neither of them saw him, for he had on the *Three-Sister Hat*.

When the princess had been with the troll a little while, and it began to grow towards dawn, she set off home again, and the companion got up behind her on the goat, and they got back fast and safe.

Next day, when the lad was called down to dinner, the companion gave him the ball. The princess was even more high and haughty than the day before, and after they had dined, she perked up her mouth and said in a dainty voice, "Perhaps it is too much to look for that you should give me back my golden ball, which I gave you to keep yesterday?"

"Is it?" asked the lad. "You shall soon have it. Here it is, safe enough." And as he said that, he threw it down on the board so hard, that it shook again; as for the king, he gave a jump high up in the air.

The princess got as pale as a corpse, but she soon came to herself again, and said, in a sweet, small voice, "Well done, well done! Now you have only one more trial left, and it is this: If you are so clever as to bring me what I am now thinking of by dinner-time tomorrow, you shall win me, and have me to wife."

From "The Companion," 1886
ARTIST: *Erik Werenskiold*

The lad felt like one doomed to death, for he thought it quite impossible to know what she was thinking about, and still harder to bring it to her; and so, when he went up to his bedroom, it was hard work to comfort himself at all. His companion told him to be easy; he would see if he could not get the right end of the stick this time too, as he had done twice before. So the lad at last took heart and lay down to sleep.

Meanwhile, the companion went to the smith and got twenty-four pounds of iron welded on his sword, and when that was done, he went down to the stable and let fly at the billygoat with such a blow, that the poor creature went right head over heels against the wall.

"When rides the princess to her lover tonight?" he asked.

"At one o'clock," baaed the billygoat.

When the hour drew near, the companion stood in the stable with his *Three-Sister Hat* on; and when the princess had greased the goat and uttered the same words that they were to fly through the air to her true love who was waiting for her in the fell, off they went again on the wings of the wind, the companion sitting behind.

But he was not light-handed this time; for, every now and then, he gave the princess a slap so that he almost beat the breath out of her body.

And when they came to the wall of rock, she knocked at the door, and it opened, and they passed on into the fell to her lover.

As soon as she got there, she fell to bewailing, and was very cross, and said she never knew the air could deal such buffets she almost thought, indeed, that someone sat behind, who beat both the billygoat and herself; she was sure she was black and blue all over her body for such a hard flight had she through the air.

Then she went on to tell how her wooer had brought her the golden ball, too. How it happened neither she nor the troll could tell.

"But now do you know what I have hit upon?"

"No, but tell me," the troll answered.

"Well," she went on, "I have told him to bring me what I was then thinking of by dinner-time tomorrow, and what I thought of was your head. Do you think he can get that, my darling?"

"No, I don't think he can," said the troll. "I would take an oath that he couldn't." And then the troll burst out laughing, and both the princess and the troll thought the lad would be drawn and quartered, and that the crows would peck out his eyes before he could get the troll's head.

So when it turned towards dawn, the princess had to set off home again; but she was afraid, she said, for she thought there was someone behind her, and so she was afraid to ride home alone. The troll must go with her on the way. The troll agreed to go along, and he led out his billygoat (for he had one that matched the princess's) and he smeared it and greased it between the horns. And when the troll got up, the companion crept up behind, and so off they set through the air to the grange. But all the way the companion thrashed the troll and his billygoat, and gave them cut and thrust and thrust and cut with his sword till they got weaker and weaker, and at last were well on the way to sink down into the sea over which they passed. Now the troll thought the weather was so wild, he went home with the princess to the grange, and stood outside to see that she got home safe and well. But as she shut the door behind her, the companion struck off the troll's head and ran up with it to the lad's room.

"Here is what the princess thought of," said he.

Well, they were merry and joyful, one may think, and when the lad was bidden down to dinner, and they had dined, the princess was as lively as a lark.

"No doubt you have got what I thought of?" said she.

"Aye, aye, I have it," said the lad, and he tore it out from under his coat, and threw it down on the board with such a thump that the board, trestles and all, was upset. As for the princess, she was as though she had been dead and buried, but she could not say that this was not what she was thinking of, and so now he was to have her to wife as she had given her word. So they made a bridal feast, and there was drinking and gladness all over the kingdom.

But the companion took the lad on one side, and told him that he might just shut his eyes and sham sleep on the bridal night; but if he held his life dear, and would listen to him, he wouldn't let a wink come over them till he had stripped her of her troll-skin, which had been thrown over her, but he must flog it off her with a rod made of nine new birch twigs, and he must tear it off her in three tubs of milk. First he was to scrub her in a tub of year-old whey, and then he was to scour her in the tub of but-termilk, and lastly, he was to rub her in a tub of new milk. The birch twigs lay under the bed, and the tubs he had set in the corner of the room. Everything was ready to his hand. Yes, the lad gave his word to do as he was bid and to listen to him. So when they got into the bridal bed that evening, the lad shammed as though he had given himself up to sleep. Then the princess raised herself up on her elbow and looked at him to see if he slept, and tickled him under the nose, but the lad slept on still. Then she tugged his hair and his beard, but he lay like a log as she thought. After that she drew out a big butcher's knife from under the bolster and was just going to hack off his head when the lad jumped up, dashed the knife out of her hand, and caught her by the hair. Then he flogged her with the birch and wore them out upon her till there was not a twig left. When that was over he tumbled her into the tub of whey, and then he got to see what sort of beast she was: she was black as a raven all over her body. But when he scrubbed her well in the whey, and scoured her with buttermilk, and rubbed her well in new milk, her troll-skin dropped off her, and she was fair and lovely and gentle; so lovely she had never looked before.

Next day the companion said they must set off home. The lad was ready enough, and the princess too, for her dower had been long waiting.

In the night the companion fetched to the grange all the gold and silver and precious things which the troll had left behind in the fell, and when they were ready to start in the morning, the whole grange was so full of silver and gold and jewels that there was no walking without treading on them. That dower was worth more than all the king's land and realm, and they were at their wits' end to know how to carry it with them. But the companion knew a way out of every strait. The troll left behind him six billygoats who could all fly through the air. Those he so loaded with silver and gold that they were forced to walk along the ground, and had no strength to mount aloft and fly, and what they could not carry had to stay behind in the king's grange. So they traveled far, and farther than far, but at last they got so footsore and tired they could not go another step. The lad and the princess knew not what to do, but when the companion saw they could not get on, he took the whole dower on his back, and the billygoats atop of it, and bore it all so far on that there was only half a mile left to the lad's home.

Then the companion said, "Now we must part, I can't stay with you any longer." But the lad would not part from him. He would not lose him for much or little. They walked on a quarter of a mile more, but farther he could not go, and when the lad begged and prayed him to go home with him, and stay with him altogether, or at least as long as they had drunk his homecoming ale in his father's house, the companion said, "No, that cannot be. Now we must part, for I hear the bells of heaven ringing for me." He was the vintner who had stood in the block of ice outside the church door, whom all spat upon, and he had been the companion and helped him because he had given all he had to get him peace and rest in Christian earth. "I had leave," he said, "to follow you a year, and now the year is out."

Soria Moria Castle

by Theodor Kittelsen
translated by Joanne Asala

One day as Espen Askeladden was poking about in the fireplace, some glowing coals rolled out from the gray ashes. They quickly formed themselves into a tiny golden castle. Askeladden could find neither peace nor rest—he thought the golden castle was so wonderful that without fail he had to find its like.

So he packed some food into his scrip and set out into the wide world in search of the castle. He traveled through forests and valleys, mountains and moors, and many blue horizons. Far, far away something was shining as brightly as a star. And as he came nearer and nearer, across a wide way, he could see that east of the sun and west of the moon lay Soria Moria Castle, shimmering in golden splendor.

Then he came to another vast forest where he met Mikkel the Fox.

"Oh, dear friend, give me something to eat. I have such a hunger that it whistles and sings within me," wailed the Fox.

"Oh, you poor thing!" said Askeladden. "Sit down and take whatever you want from my scrip."

"God bless you, dear friend," said Mikkel.

Deeper into the wild wood went Askeladden, and there he met Bamse the Bear.

"Oh, my kind boy, please give me something to eat!" growled the Bear. "I'm so hungry that my stomach rumbles and roars!"

"Well," said Askeladden, "I haven't much left, but we can share what I have, since your need is great."

"That is kind of you, you have my thanks," said the Bear. "You don't need to worry, I won't eat it all."

It grew darker and darker. Two green eyes shone brightly from the trees. It was Iserim, the Wolf.

"Whoo! Whoo!" he howled. "I want something to eat! I want something to eat! I'm so terribly hungry that it pulls and tears, howls and hoots in my intestines. Whoo!"

"Well," said Askeladden. "We can share the few crumbs I have left in my scrip. I'm sorry I can't do better."

"Whoo! Then I won't have to eat *you* for supper," howled the Wolf.

Askeladden wandered far, and farther than far, over moors and mountains. Then something big and heavy rose before him so that the earth itself trembled and shook. It was an enormous troll, and he was in search of some good Christian folk for his supper.

Askeladden was no longer weighed down by his scrip or a full stomach, so he easily jumped over boulders and logs, and disappeared in the bushes.

From "Soria Moria Castle," retold by Andrew Lang, 1890
ARTIST: *H.J. Ford*

At last he stood before Soria Moria Castle. It towered over him like a mountain of glittering gold amidst the swirling clouds. It was unnaturally quiet, and Askeladden could not help but wonder why. Surely some poor princess was trapped inside! He had to go in and set her free. If only he could find his way through the fog and mist!

Guarding the outside of the castle was a many-headed dragon. It had slept for a hundred thousand years. Its rough, weather-worn hide was covered in lichen, moss, and grass. Its closed eyes were set deep in its skull. Askeladden was frightened, but he crept carefully past the hideous beast, which slept like a log.

Just outside the castle stood a golden linden tree in which sat a sleeping golden bird, shining like the sun. For a hundred thousand years it had slept. The bird was so beautiful that Askeladden wished to touch it, but then Askeladden remembered the sleeping dragon. If the bird cried out, it might wake the dragon. Askeladden crept silently past it to the castle gate.

The doors stood wide open, and there sat a princess scratching the heads of a big, ugly troll.

"Oh, my heavens!" said the princess. "Does a Christian man dare come here?"

"It has happened," said Askeladden.

"When the troll wakes up, he'll eat both hide and hair of you!" said the princess. "Hurry and drink from that horn over there, until you can swing the great sword that stands in the corner."

Askeladden took a great draught from the bottle, and he was able to swing the sword as if it were light as a feather. Just then the troll woke up.

"What's this I smell?" he roared. "Christian blood?"

"Yes!" cried Askeladden. "But it's the last thing you'll smell!" With that he cut off the ugly heads of the troll. You can well imagine Askeladden's joy! The princess, her kingdom, and all of the gold and silver in Soria Moria Castle were now his.

Nobody has ever seen a wedding that can match theirs. The king himself was there, along with the parson and the sexton, the Bear, the Wolf and the Fox, and yes, even the local gypsy woman. There was so much noise and laughter that it could be heard twelve kingdoms away. And if you don't believe this, you can go and ask the people who were there.

The Troll and Dyre
ARTIST: *Theodor Kittelsen*

Dyre Vaa and the Mountain Troll

by Theodor Kittelsen
translated by Joanne Asala

Over in Telemark, under the tall and mighty mountains of Rauland, there is a great mountain lake known as Totak, which rarely freezes before Christmas. On the shores of this lake is Vå, a farm where there once lived a man named Dyre. He was known far and wide for not being afraid of anything.

Late one Christmas Eve the people of Vå heard a horrendous howling coming from the other side of the lake. Everyone quaked in fright; everyone, that is, except Dyre. He walked calmly down to the water's edge to discover what was going on.

He took his skiff and rowed across to where the sounds were coming from. It was as black as pitch, but he could tell that the hollering came from a huge mountain troll, even though he couldn't see him.

"Who are you?" demanded the troll.

"I am Dyre Vaa," he answered. "Where do you come from?"

"From Åshaug," came the reply.

"And where are you going now?"

"To Glomshaug, to my maidens. Will you sail me across?"

Dyre agreed to do so, but when the troll set his foot in the boat it nearly sank. "Make yourself lighter, you great lump!" Dyre Vaa shouted.

"Yes, all right, I will do so," answered the troll. "I'll make myself lighter." So Dyre Vaa began to row the troll across the lake.

"Let me see how big you are," said Dyre.

"No, I don't have time for that," said the troll. "But I'll leave behind a sign in your boat."

Early on Christmas morning Dyre Vaa went down to the shore to look for the promised sign. In the boat he found the thumb belonging to the troll's mitten. He dragged it home in order to measure it, and it was hardly small! It held two heaping bushels full of grain.

The Battle of the Giants

by Theodor Kittelsen
translated by Joanne Asala

From high up on the mountaintop everything looks small. In the deep, awe-inspiring stillness, thoughts sail on widespread wings. When the evening sun casts its glow from peak to peak, it is as if some great silent god is wandering about, searching with his enormous lamp.

Overhead churn the dark storm clouds; the icy wind sweeps over the valley, asking in a thousand voices, "Where to? Where to?"

What is this loud din that pierces the silence?

The sky turns black. Millions of raindrops splatter and hiss, as if all of the heavens have opened at once. Crackling lightning streaks from cloud to cloud . . . echoing wildly between the mountains. From the darkness a voice is heard:

"I am the Master of Jotunheimen!"

Two giants emerge from the mists in a furious struggle across the jagged mountaintops. The mountains tremble, rockslides thunder. Pools of blood remain like wild mountain lakes, black and deep!

More rain falls from the sky in a cascading stream. Thunder booms, like planets colliding, and the lightning crashes, flash after flash. Now Thor is throwing his hammer at Jotunheimen! Run for cover! Run for cover! The reindeer come charging in disarray; how the stones fly from their hooves! Clip-clop! Clip-clop! Run for cover!

The sky turns as dark as a grave. Among the mountains the furious giants rumble about until Thor's hammer sends them into the shadows.

A soft, gentle rain begins to fall. Tinkling voices murmur from crevices and hollows, telling all who will listen of the noisy events. In the silent dark they merge in a humming chorus—rustling yellow leaves fall from the tree of life.

Far, far away, over the wide valley, a deep, growling voice is still to be heard: "I am the Master of Jotunheimen. Alone will I be. Do not disturb my peace!"

East o' the Sun and West o' the Moon

by Peter Christian Asbjørnsen
translated by George Webbe Dasent

Once on a time there was a poor husbandman who had so many children that he hadn't much of either food or clothing to give them. Pretty children they all were, but the prettiest was the youngest daughter, who was so lovely there was no end to her loveliness.

So one day, 'twas on a Thursday evening late at the fall of the year, the weather was so wild and rough outside, and it was so cruelly dark, and rain fell and wind blew till the walls of the cottage shook. There they all sat round the fire busy with this thing and that. But just then, all at once something gave three taps on the windowpane. Then the father went out to see what was the matter, and when he got out of doors, what should he see but a great big White Bear.

From "East of the Sun and West of the Moon," 1889
ARTIST: *H.J. Ford*

"Good evening to you," said the White Bear.

"The same to you," said the man.

"Will you give me your youngest daughter? If you will, I'll make you as rich as you are now poor," said the Bear.

Well, the man would not be at all sorry to be so rich, but still he thought he must have a bit of a talk with his daughter first; so he went in and told them how there was a great White Bear waiting outside who had given his word to make them so rich if he could only have the youngest daughter.

The lassie said "No!" outright. Nothing could get her to say anything else; so the man went out and settled it with the White Bear, that he should come again the next Thursday evening and get an answer. Meantime he talked it over with his daughter, and kept telling her of all the riches they would get, and how well off she would be herself. At last she thought better of it, and washed and mended her rags, made herself as smart as she could, and was ready to start. I can't say her packing gave her much trouble.

Next Thursday evening came the White Bear to fetch her, and she got upon his back with her bundle, and off they went. So, when they had gone a bit of the way, the White Bear said, "Are you afraid?"

"No," she said in a small voice.

"Well, mind that you hold tight to my shaggy coat, and then there's nothing to fear," said the Bear.

So she rode a long, long way, till they came to a great steep hill. There, on the face of it, the White Bear gave a knock, and a door opened, and they came into a castle where there were many rooms all lit up, rooms gleaming with silver and gold, and there, too, was a table ready laid, and it was all as grand as grand could be. Then the White Bear gave her a silver bell, and when she wanted anything, she was only to ring it, and she would get it at once.

After she had eaten and drunk her fill, she grew sleepy and thought she would like to go to bed, and so she rang the bell. Scarce had she taken hold of it before she was brought to a chamber where there was a bed made, as fair and white as anyone would wish to sleep on, with silken pillows and curtains and gold fringe. All that was in the room was gold or silver. But when she had gone to bed and put out the light, a man came and laid himself alongside her. That was the White Bear, who threw off his beast shape at night, but she never saw him, for he always came after she had put out the light, and before the day dawned he was up and off again.

So things went on happily for awhile, but at last she began to get silent and sorrowful; for there she went about all day alone, and she longed to go home to see her father and mother, and brothers and sisters. So one day, when the White Bear asked what it was that she lacked, she said it was so dull and lonely there, and she longed to go home to see her father and mother, and brothers and sisters, and that was why she was so sad and sorrowful, because she couldn't get to them.

"Well, well!" said the Bear. "Perhaps there's a cure for all this, but you must promise me one thing: not to talk with your mother, but only when the rest are by to hear; for she'll take you by the hand and try to lead you into a room alone to talk. You must mind and not do that, else you'll bring bad luck on both of us."

So one Sunday the White Bear came and said now they could set off to see her father and mother. Well, off they started, she sitting on his back, and they went far and long. At last they came to a grand house, and there her brothers and sisters were running about out-of-doors at play, and everything was so pretty 'twas a joy to see.

"This is where your father and mother live now," said the White Bear. "But don't forget what I told you, else you'll make us both unlucky."

"No! I will not forget," she said when she reached the house, and the White Bear turned right about and left her.

When she went in to see her father and mother, there was such joy; there was no end to it. None of them thought they could thank her enough for all she had done for them. Now they had everything they wished, as good as good could be, and they all wanted to know how she got on where she lived.

"Well," she said, "it is very good to live where I do. I have all that I could wish for." What she said beside I don't know, but I don't think any of them had the right end of the stick, or that they got much out of her. So in the afternoon, after they had done dinner, all happened as the White Bear had said. Her mother wanted to talk with her alone in her bedroom, but she minded what the White Bear said, and wouldn't go upstairs.

"Oh, what we have to talk about will keep," she said, and put her mother off. But somehow or other, her mother got round her at last, and she had to tell her the whole story. "Every night, when I have gone to bed, a man comes and lays down beside me as soon as I put out the light. I never see him because he is always up and away before the morning dawns. My days are long and lonely and very dull. I would like to see him just once, just to know what he looks like."

"My!" said her mother. "It may well be a troll you sleep with! But now I'll teach you a lesson how to set eyes on him. I'll give you a bit of candle which you can carry home in your bosom; just light that while he is asleep, but take care not to drop the tallow on him."

So the girl took the candle, and hid it in her bosom, and as night drew on, the White Bear came and fetched her away. But when they had gone a bit of the way, the White Bear asked if all hadn't happened as he had said.

"Well, I can't say it hadn't."

"Now mind," he said, "if you have listened to your mother's advice, you have brought bad luck on us both, and then all that has passed between us will be as nothing."

"No," she said, "I didn't listen to my mother's advice."

When she reached home and had gone to bed, it was the old story all over again. There came a man who lay down beside her, but at dead of night, when she heard he slept, she got up and struck a light, lit the candle and let the light shine on him, and so she saw that he was the loveliest prince one ever set eyes on, and she fell so deep in love with him on the very spot that she thought she couldn't live if she didn't give him a kiss then and there. And so she did just that, but as she kissed him, she dropped three hot drops of tallow on his shirt, and he woke up.

"What have you done?" he cried. "Now you have made us both unlucky, for had you held out only this one year, I would have been free. I have a stepmother who has bewitched me so that I am a White Bear by day and a man by night. But now all ties are snapped between us; now I must set off from you to her. She lives in a castle which stands East of the Sun and West of the Moon, and there, too, is a princess, with a nose three ells long, and she's the wife I must have now."

She wept and took it ill, but there was no help for it; go he must.

Then she asked if she mightn't go with him. "No you may not," he said.

"Tell me the way, then," she begged, "and I'll search you out. That surely I may get leave to do."

"Yes, you may do that," he said, "but there is no way to that place. It lies East of the Sun and West of the Moon, and thither you'll never find your way."

From "East of the Sun and West of the Moon," 1889
ARTIST: *H.J. Ford*

So next morning, when she woke up, both prince and castle were gone, and then she lay on a little green patch in the midst of the gloomy thick wood, and by her side lay the same bundle of rags she had brought with her from her old home.

When she had rubbed the sleep out of her eyes and wept till she was tired, she set out on her way and walked many, many days, till she came to a lofty crag. Under it sat an old troll hag who played with a golden apple. The girl asked if she knew the way to the prince who lived with his step-mother in the castle that lay East of the Sun and West of the Moon, and who was to marry the princess with a nose three ells long.

"How did you come to know about him?" asked the old hag. "Maybe you are the lass who ought to have had him?"

"Yes, I am," said the girl sadly.

"So, so, it's you, is it?" said the old hag. "Well, all I know about him is that he lives in the castle that lies East of the Sun and West of the Moon, and thither you'll come, late or never. Still, you may have the loan of my horse, and on him you can ride to my next neighbor. Maybe she'll be able to tell you, and when you get there, just give the horse a switch under the left ear, and beg him to be off home, and this golden apple you may take with you."

So the girl got up on the horse, and rode a long, long time till she came to another crag, under which sat another hag with a gold carding comb. The lassie asked if she knew the way to the castle that lay East of the Sun and West of the Moon, and the hag answered, like the first old hag, that she knew nothing about it, except it was East of the Sun and West of the Moon. "And thither you'll come, late or never, but you shall have loan of my horse to my next neighbor, maybe she'll tell you all about it, and when you get there, just switch the horse under the left ear, and beg him to be off home."

And this old hag gave her the golden carding comb; it might be she'd find some use for it, she said. So the lassie got up on the horse, and rode far, and farther than far, and had a weary time of it, and so at last she came to another great crag, under which sat another old hag, spinning with a golden spinning wheel. The girl asked if she knew the way to the prince and where the castle was that lay East of the Sun and West of the Moon. So it was the same thing over again.

"Maybe it's you who ought to have had the prince?" asked the old hag.

"Yes, I am the one."

But she, too, didn't know the way a bit better than the other two. "East of the Sun and West of the Moon it was," that was all she knew. "And thither you'll come, late or never, but I'll lend you my horse, and then I think you'd best ride to the East Wind and ask him. Maybe he knows those parts, and can blow you thither. But when you get to him, you need only give the horse a switch under the left ear, and he'll trot home of himself."

And so, too, she gave the girl her gold spinning wheel. "Maybe you'll find a use for it," said the old hag.

Then on she rode many, many days, a weary time, before she got to the East Wind's house. At last she did reach it, and then she asked the East Wind if he could tell her the way to the prince who dwelt East of the Sun and West of the Moon. The East Wind had often heard tell of it, the prince and the castle, but he couldn't tell the way for he had never blown so far.

"But, if you will, I'll go with you to my brother the West Wind, maybe he knows for he's much stronger. So, if you will just get on my back, I'll carry you thither."

So she got on his back, and I should think they went briskly along. When they got there, they went into the West Wind's house, and the East Wind said the lassie he had brought was the one who ought to have had the prince who lived in the castle East of the Sun and West of the Moon, and so she had set out to seek him, and how he had come with her, and would be glad to know if the West Wind knew how to get to the castle.

"No," said the West Wind, "so far I've never blown, but if you will, I'll go with you to our brother the South Wind, for he's much stronger than either of us, and he has flapped his wings far and wide. Maybe he'll tell you. You can get on my back, and I'll carry you to him."

Yes! She got on his back, and so they traveled to the South Wind, and weren't so very long on the way, I should think.

When they got there, the West Wind asked him if he could tell her the way to the castle that lay East of the Sun and West of the Moon, for it was she who ought to have had the prince who lived there.

"You don't say! That's she, is it?" asked the South Wind. "Well, I have blustered about in most places in my time, but so far have I never blown, but if you will, I'll take you to my brother the North Wind; he is the oldest and strongest of the whole lot of us, and if he doesn't know where it is, you'll never find anyone in the world to tell you. You can get on my back, and I'll carry you thither."

So she got on the back of the South Wind, and away he went from his home at a fine rate. And this time, too, she wasn't long on her way.

So when they got to the North Wind's house, he was so wild and cross, cold puffs came from him a long way off.

"Blast you both, what do you want?" he roared out to them ever so far off, so that it struck them with an icy shiver.

"Well," said the South Wind, "you needn't be so foulmouthed, for here I am, your brother the South Wind, and here is the lassie who ought to have had the prince who dwells in the castle East of the Sun and West of the Moon, and now she wants to ask you if you ever were there, and can tell her the way, for she would be so glad to find him again."

From "East of the Sun and West of the Moon," 1889
ARTIST: *H.J. Ford*

"Yes, I know well enough where it is," said the North Wind. "Once in my life I blew an aspen leaf thither, but I was so tired I couldn't blow a puff for ever so many days after. But if you really wish to go thither, and aren't afraid to come along with me, I'll take you on my back and see if I can blow you thither."

"Yes! With all my heart I wish to go. As for fear, however madly you go, I won't be afraid."

"Very well then," said the North Wind, "but you must sleep here tonight, for we must have the whole day before us, if we're thinking to get there at all."

Early the next morning the North Wind woke her and puffed himself up and blew himself out, and made himself so stout and big 'twas gruesome to look at him. So off they went high up through the air, as if they would never stop till they got to the world's end.

Down below there was such a storm it threw down long tracts of wood and many houses, and when it swept over the great sea, ships foundered by hundreds.

So they tore on and on—no one can believe how far they went—and all the while they still went over the sea, and the North Wind got more and more weary, and so out of breath he could scarce bring out a puff, and his wings drooped and drooped till at last he sunk so low that the crests of the waves dashed over his heels.

"Are you afraid?" asked the North Wind.

"No, I'm not," said the girl.

"I believe you're lying, for I'm a little nervous myself," chuckled the North Wind.

But they weren't very far from land, and the North Wind had still enough strength left in him that he managed to throw her up on the shore under the windows of the castle which lay East of the Sun and West of the Moon; but he was so weak and worn out, he had to stay there and rest many days before he could get home again.

Next morning the lassie sat down under the castle window and began to play with the gold apple, and the first person she saw was the long-nose who was to have the prince.

"What do you want for your gold apple, girl?" asked the long-nose, and threw up the window.

"Oh, it's not for sale, for gold or money," said the lassie.

"If it's not for sale for gold or money, what is it that you will sell it for? You may name your own price," said the troll princess.

"Well, if I may get to the prince, who lives here, and be with him tonight, you shall have it," said the lassie whom the North Wind had brought.

The princess agreed to that, and so got the golden apple. But when the lassie came up to the prince's bedroom at night, she found him fast asleep. She called and shook him, and between whiles she wept sore, but for all she could do she couldn't wake him up. Next morning, as soon as day broke, came the princess with the long nose, and drove her out again.

So in the daytime she sat down under the castle windows and began to card with her golden carding comb, and the same thing happened. The princess asked what she wanted for it, and she said it wasn't for sale for gold or money, but if she might get leave to go up to the prince and be with him that night, the princess should have it. But when she went up she found him fast asleep again, and all she called, and all she shook, and wept, and prayed, she couldn't get life into him, and as soon as the first gray peep of day came, then came the princess with the long nose, and chased her out again.

So in the daytime the lassie sat down outside under the castle window, and began to spin with her golden spinning wheel, and that, too, the princess with the long nose wanted to have. So she threw up the window and asked what she wanted for it. The lassie said, as she had said twice before, it wasn't for sale for gold or money, but if she might go up to the prince who was there, and be with him alone that night, she might have it.

Yes! She might do that and welcome. But now you must know there were some Christian folk who had been carried off thither, and as they sat in their room which was next to the prince, they had heard how a woman had been in there, and wept and prayed, and called to him two nights running, and they told that to the prince.

That evening, when the princess came with her sleepy drink, the prince made as if he drank, but threw it over his shoulder, for he could guess it was a sleepy drink. So, when the lassie came in, she found the prince wide awake, and then she told him the whole story of how she had come thither.

"Ah," said the prince, "you've just come in the very nick of time, for tomorrow is to be my wedding day. Now I won't have the long-nose, and you are the only woman in the world who can set me free. I'll say I want to see what my wife is fit for, and beg her to wash the shirt which has the three spots of tallow on it. She'll say yes, for she doesn't know 'tis you who put them there. That's a work only for Christian folk, and not for such a pack of trolls; and so I'll say that I won't have any other for my bride than the woman who can wash them out, and ask you to do it."

So there was great joy and love between them all that night. But next day, when the wedding was to be, the prince said, "First of all, I'd like to see what my bride is fit for."

"Yes!" said the stepmother. "With all my heart."

"Well," said the prince, "I've got a fine shirt which I'd like for my wedding shirt, but somehow or other it has got three spots of tallow on it, which I must have washed out, and I have sworn never to take any other for my bride than the woman who's able to do that. If she can't accomplish the task, she's not worth having."

Well, that was no great thing, they said, so they agreed, and she with the long-nose began to wash away as hard as she could, but the more she rubbed and scrubbed, the bigger the spots grew.

"Ah!" said the old hag, her mother, "you can't wash. Let me try."

But she hadn't long taken the shirt in hand, before it got far worse than ever, and with all her rubbing and wringing and scrubbing, the spots grew bigger and blacker, and the darker and uglier the shirt.

Then all the other trolls began to wash, but the longer it lasted, the blacker and uglier the shirt grew, till at last it was as black all over as if it had been up the chimney.

"Ah," said the prince, "you're none of you worth a straw. You can't wash. Why there, outside, sits a beggar lassie; I'll be bound she knows how to wash better than the whole lot of you. Come in, lassie!" he shouted.

Well, in she came.

"Can you wash this shirt clean, lassie, you?" said he.

"I don't know," she said, "but I think I can." And almost before she had taken it and dipped it in the water, it was as white as driven snow, and whiter still.

"Yes, you are the lassie for me," said the prince.

At that the old hag flew into such a rage, she burst on the spot, and the princess with the long nose after her, and the whole pack of trolls after her, at least I've never heard a word about them since. As for the prince and his new princess, they set free all the poor Christian folk who had been carried off and shut up there, and they took with them all the silver and gold, and flitted away as fast as they could from the castle that lay East of the Sun and West of the Moon.

Jonas Lie

The Darker Side of Human Nature

The great nineteenth-century writer Jonas Lie admitted to having a twilight nature. He used his shorter stories as a vehicle for exploring the possibility that within each one of us there is a dark, twisted troll waiting to be freed.

Lie was born on November 6, 1833, at Hougsund, Eker, just outside of Kristiania (modern-day Oslo), Norway. At the age of five he moved with his family to the city of Tromsø, where he came under the influence of the haunting countryside of the north, described by Alrik Gustafson as a "kaleidoscopic shifting of landscape effects, its lurid intensities of light and darkness, its eternal night of winter and continuous day of summer, its fantastic world of darksome superstitions."

In 1880 Lie wrote, "It is part of my observation of life [that there is] a discrepancy between intellectual development and moral ignorance that can manifest itself in one and the same person. Passion, this wild beast within man, breaks out the moment he least expects it, for he is not practiced in controlling it." In 1890 he furthered his ideas by saying, "Might there not be a little, exciting, incalculable troll concealed somewhere deep within?"

Many of Lie's stories have a "folkish" tone to them, and certainly he must have been aware of the work of Peter Asbjørnsen and Jørgen Moe. While some of Lie's tales are told in the simplistic, unadorned manner of the folktale medium, others are quite poetic, carefully weaving a moral lesson for the reader.

"That there are trolls in human beings everyone knows who has an eye for that kind of thing," Lie wrote. "They lie within the personality and bind it like the immovable part of a mountain, like a capricious sea and uncontrollable weather. Trolldom lives inside mankind as temperament, natural will, and explosive power." Lie hoped to show mankind that by recognizing this nature, we could separate ourselves from it, and rise above our troll-like impulses.

ARTIST: *Laurence Housman*

The Wind Troll

by Jonas Lie
translated by R. Nisbet Bain

There was once a skipper of Dyrevig called Bardun. He was so headstrong that there was no doing anything with him. Whatever he set his mind upon, that should be done, he said, and done it always was.

If he promised to be at a dance, the girls could safely rely upon his being there, though it blew a tempest and rained cats and dogs.

He would come scudding along on a færing, a small two-oared boat, to his father's house through storm and stress. Row upon row of girls would be waiting for him there, and he spanked the floor with every one of them in turn, and left their gallants to cool their heels as best they might.

Cock-of-the-walk he always must be.

He would go shark fishing, too, and would venture with his fishing gaff into seas where only large ships were wont to go.

If there was anything nobody else dared do, Bardun was the man to do it. And, absurd and desperate as the venture might be, he always succeeded, so that folks were always talking about him.

Now, right out at sea, beyond the skerries, lay a large rock, the lair of wild fowl, where the merchant who owned it came every year to bring away rich loads of eiderdown. A long way down the side of this lofty rock was a cleft. Nobody could tell how far into the rock it went, and so inaccessible was it there that its owner had said that whoever liked might come and take eiderdown from there. It became quite a proverb to say, when anything couldn't get done, that it was "just as impossible as taking eiderdown from Dyrevig rock."

But Bardun passed by the rock, and peeped up at the cleft, and saw all the hosts of the fowls of the air lighting upon it so many times that he felt he must try his hand at it.

He lost no time about it, and the sun was shining brightly as he set out.

He took with him a long piece of rope, which he cast two or three times round a rocky crag, and lowered himself down till he was right opposite the cleft. There he hung and swung over it backward and forward till he had gotten a firm footing, and then he set about collecting eiderdown and stuffing his sacks with it.

He went searching about for it so far into the rocky chasm that he saw no more than a gleam of sunlight outside the opening, and he couldn't take a hundredth part of the eiderdown that was there.

It was quite late in the evening before he gave up trying to gather it all. But when he came out again, the stone which he had placed on the top of the rope and tied it to was gone. And now the rope hung loosely there and dangled over the side of the rock. The wind blew it in and out and hither and there. The currents of air sported madly with it, so that it always kept sheer away from the rock and far out over the abyss.

There he stood then, and tried again and again to clutch hold of it till the sun lay right down in the sea.

When it began to dawn again, and the morning breeze rose up from the sea, he all at once heard something right over his head say—

"It blows away, it blows away!"

He looked up, and there he saw a big woman holding the rope away from the cliff side.

Every time he made a grip at it she wrenched and twisted it right away over the rocky wall, and there was a laughing and a grinning all down the mountain side—

"It blows away, it blows away!"

And, again and again, the rope drove in and out and hither and thither.

"You had better take a spring at once and not wait till you're tired," thought he.

It was a pretty long leap to take, but he went back a sufficient distance, and then out he sprang.

Bardun was not the man to fall short of anything. He caught the rope and held it tight.

And, oddly enough, it seemed now to run up the cliff-side of its own accord, just as if someone were hoisting it.

But in front of the rocky crag to which he had fastened the rope, he heard a soughing and a sighing, and something said, "I am the daughter of the Wind Troll, and now you have dominion over me! When the blast blows and whines about you, it is I who longs for you. And here you have a rudder which will give you luck and a fair wind wherever you go. He who is with you shall thrive, and he who is against you shall suffer shipwreck and be lost. For 'tis I who am in the windy gusts."

Then all at once everything was quite still, but down on the sea below there swept a heavy squall.

There stood Bardun with the rudder in his hand, and he understood that it was not a thing to be lightly cast away.

Homeward he steered with a racing breeze behind him, and he had not sailed far before he met a galeas which gave him the Bergen price for his eiderdown.

But Bardun was not content with only going there once. He went just the same as before, and he returned from the Dyrevig rock with a pile of sacks of eiderdown on his boat right up to the mast.

He bought houses and ships; mightier he grew.

And it was not long before he owned whole fishing grounds, both northwards and southwards.

Those who submitted to him, and did as he would have them do, increased and prospered and saw good days, but all who stood in his way were wrecked on the sea and perished, for the Wind Troll was on his side.

So things quickly went from good to better with him. What was to him a fair wind was the ruin of all those who were in any way opposed to him. At last he became so rich and mighty that he owned every blessed trading place and fishing station in all Finmark, and sent vessels even as far as Spitzbergen.

Nobody dared sell fish up north without his leave, and his sloops sailed over to Bergen eighteen at a time.

He ruled and gave judgment as it seemed best to him.

But the magistrates thought that such authority was too much for one man to have, and they began to make inquiries and receive complaints of how he domineered the people.

Next, the magistrates sent him a warning.

"But the right to rule lies in my rudder," thought Bardun to himself.

Then the magistrates summoned him before the tribunal.

Bardun simply whistled contemptuously.

At last matters came to such a pitch that the magistrates sailed forth to seize him in the midst of a howling tempest, and down they went in the Finmark seas.

Then Bardun was made chief magistrate till such time as the king should send up another.

But the new man who came had not been very long in office there before it seemed to him as if it was not he but Bardun who held sway.

So the same thing happened over again.

Bardun was summoned in vain before the courts, and the magistrates came forth to seize him and perished at sea.

But when the next governor was sent up to Finmark, it was only the keel of the king's ship that came drifting in from the sea. At last nobody would venture there to certain ruin, and Bardun was left alone and ruled over all. Then so mighty was he in all Finmark that he reigned there like the king himself.

Now he had but one child, and that a daughter.

Boel was her name, and she shot up so handsome and comely that her beauty shone like the sun. No bridegroom was good enough for her, unless, perhaps, it were the king's son.

Wooers came from afar, and came in vain. She was to have a dower, they said, such as no girl in the North had ever had before.

One year quite a young officer came up thither with a letter from the king. His garments were stiff with gold, and shone and sparkled wherever he went. Bardun received him well, and helped him to carry out the king's commands.

But since the day when he himself was young, and got the answer, "Yes!" from his bride, he had never been so happy as when Boel came to him one day and said that the young officer had wooed her, and she would throw herself into the sea straightway if she couldn't have him.

In this way, he argued, his race would always sit in the seat of authority and hold sway when he was gone.

While the officer, in the course of the summer, was out on circuit, Bardun set a hundred men to work to build a house for them.

It was to shine like a castle, and be bright with high halls and large reception rooms, and windows in long rooms, and furs and cloth of gold and bright tiles were fetched from the far South.

And in the autumn there was such a wedding that the whole land heard and talked about it.

But it was not long before Bardun began to find that to be a fact which was already a rumor, to wit, that the man who had got his daughter would fain have his own way also.

He laid down the law, and gave judgment like Bardun himself, and he overruled Bardun, not once but twice.

Then Bardun went to Boel, and bade her take her husband to task, and look sharp about it. He had never yet seen the man, he said, who couldn't set right by his bride in the days when they did nothing but eat honey together.

But Boel said that she had wedded a man who, to her mind, was no less a man than her own father, and it was his office, besides, to uphold the law and jurisdiction of the king.

Young folks are easy to talk over, thought Bardun. One can do anything with them when one only makes them fancy they are having their own way. And it is wonderful how far one can get if one only bides one's time, and makes the best of things. Whatever was out of gear he could very easily put right again, when once he got a firm grip of the reins.

So he praised everything his son-in-law did, and talked big about him, so that there was really no end to it. He was glad, he said, that such a wise and stately ruler was there, ready to stand in his shoes against the day when he should grow old.

And so he made himself small, and his voice quivered when he spoke, as if he were really a sick and broken-down man. But it didn't escape Boel how he slammed to the doors and struck the stones with his stick till the sparks flew.

Next time the court met, Bardun was taxed to a full tenth of the value of all his property, according to the king's law and justice. Then only did he begin to foresee that it might fare with the magistrate now as it had done formerly.

But all women like pomp and show, thought he, and Boel was in this respect no different to other people. And she was no daughter of his, either, if she couldn't keep the upper hand of her husband.

So he bought her gold and jewels and other costly things. One day he came with a bracelet, and another day with a chain and now it was a belt, and now a gold embroidered shoe. And every time he told her that he brought her these gifts because she was his dearest jewel. He knew of nothing in the world that was too precious for her.

Then, in his most pleasant, most courtly style, he just hinted that she might see to it, and talk her husband over to other ways.

But it booted him even less than before.

And so things went on till autumn. The king's law was first, and his will was only second.

Then he began to dread what would be the end of it all. His eyes sparkled so fiercely that none dare come near him. But at night he would pace up and down, and shriek and bellow at his daughter, and give her all sorts of vile names.

Now one day he came in to Boel with a heavy crown full of the most precious stones. She should be the Queen of Finmark and Spitzbergen, said he, if her husband would do according to his will.

Then she looked him stiffly in the face, and said she would never seduce her husband into breaking the king's law. He grew as pale as the wall behind him, and cast the gold crown on the floor, so that there was a perfect shower of precious stones about them. She must know, said he, that her father and none other was king here. And now the young officer should find out how it fared with them who sat in his seat.

Then Boel washed her hands of her father altogether, but she advised her husband to depart immediately. And on the third day she had packed up all her bridal finery, and departed in the vessel with the young officer.

Then Bardun struck his head against the wall, and that night he laughed, so that it was heard far away, but he wept for his daughter.

And now there arose such a storm that the sea was white for a whole week. It was not long before the tidings came that the ship that Boel and her husband had sailed by had gone down, and the splinters lay and floated among the skerries.

Bardun took the rudder he had got from the Wind Troll, and stuck it into the stern of the largest yacht he had. He was God himself now, said he, and could always get a fair wind to steer by, and could rule where he would in the wide world. And southwards he sailed with a rattling breeze, and the billows rolled after him like mounds and hillocks.

Heavier and heavier grew the sea, till it rolled like white mountains as high as the rocky walls of Lofoten.

It couldn't well be less when he was to rule the whole world, cried he. And so he set his rudder dead southwards.

He never diminished his sail one bit, and worse and worse grew the storm, and higher and higher rose the sea.

For now he was steering right into the sun.

Finn Blood

by Jonas Lie
translated by R. Nisbet Bain

In Svartfjord, north of Senje, dwelt a lad called Eilert. His neighbors were sea-faring Finns, and among their children was a pale little girl, remarkable for her long black hair and her large eyes. They dwelt behind the crag on the other side of the promontory, and fished for a livelihood, as also did Eilert's parents; wherefore there was no particular good will between the families, for the nearest fishing ground was but a small one, and each would have liked to have rowed there alone.

Nevertheless, though his parents didn't like it at all, and even forbade it, Eilert used to sneak regularly down to the Finns. There they had always strange tales to tell, and he heard wondrous things about the recesses of the mountains, where the original home of the Finns was, and where, in the olden time, dwelt the Finn Kings, who were masters among the magicians. There, too, he heard tell of all that was beneath the sea, where the Sea Huldrer and Draug hold sway. The latter are gloomy, evil powers, and many a time his blood stood still in his veins as he sat and listened. They told him that the Draug usually showed himself on the strand in the moonlight on those spots which were covered with sea wrack; that he had a bunch of seaweed instead of a head, but shaped so peculiarly that whoever came across him absolutely couldn't help gazing into his pale and horrible face. They themselves had seen him many a time, and once they had driven him, thwart by thwart, out of the boat where he had sat one morning, and turned the oars upside down. When Eilert hastened homeward in the darkness round the headland, along the strand, over heaps of seaweed, he dared scarcely look around him, and many a time the sweat absolutely streamed from his forehead.

In proportion as hostility increased among the old people, they had a good deal of fault to find with one another, and Eilert heard no end of evil things spoken about the Finns at home. Now it was this, and now it was that. They didn't even row like honest folk, for, after the Finnish fashion, they took high and swift strokes, as if they were womenkind, and they all talked together, and made a noise while they rowed instead of being silent in the boat. But what impressed Eilert most of all was the fact that, in the

Finn woman's family, they practiced sorcery and idolatry, or so folks said. He also heard tell of something beyond all question, and that was the shame of having Finn blood in one's veins, which also was the reason why the Finns were not as good as other honest folk, so that the magistrates gave them their own distinct burial ground in the churchyard, and their own separate "Finn-pens" in church. Eilert had seen this with his own eyes in the church at Berg.

All this made him very angry, for he could not help liking the Finn folks down yonder, and especially little Zilla. They two were always together: she knew such a lot about the Sea-Huldre. Henceforth his conscience always plagued him when he played with her, and whenever she stared at him with her large black eyes while she told him tales, he used to begin to feel a little bit afraid, for at such times he reflected that she and her people belonged to the Damned, and that was why they knew so much about such things. But, on the other hand, the thought of it made him so bitterly angry, especially on her account. She, too, was frequently taken aback by his odd behavior toward her, which he couldn't understand at all and then, as was her wont, she would begin laughing at and teasing him by making him run after her, while she went and hid herself.

One day he found her sitting on a boulder by the seashore. She had in her lap an eider duck which had been shot, and could only have died quite recently, for it was still warm, and she wept bitterly over it. It was, she sobbed, the same bird which made its nest every year beneath the shelter of their outhouse. She knew it quite well, and she showed him a red-colored feather in its white breast. It had been struck dead by a single shot, and only a single red drop had come out of it; it had tried to reach its nest, but had died on its way on the strand. She wept as if her heart would break, and dried her face with her hair in impetuous Finn fashion. Eilert laughed at her as boys will, but he overdid it, and was very pale the whole time. He dared not tell her that that very day he had taken a random shot with his father's gun from behind the headland at a bird a long way off which was swimming ashore.

One autumn Eilert's father was downright desperate. Day after day on the fishing grounds his lines caught next to nothing, while he was forced to look on and see the Finn pull up one rich catch after another. He was sure, too, that he had noticed malicious gestures over the Finn's boat. After that his whole house nourished a double bitterness against them, and when they talked it over in the evening, it was agreed, as a thing beyond all question, that Finnish sorcery had something to do with it. Against this there was only one remedy, and that was to rub corpse-mold on the lines; but one must beware of doing so, lest one should thereby offend the dead and expose oneself to their vengeance, while the sea-folk would gain power over one at the same time.

Eilert bothered his head a good deal over all this; it almost seemed to him as if he had had a share in the deed, because he was on such a good footing with the Finn folks.

On the following Sunday, both he and the Finn folks were at Berg church, and he secretly abstracted a handful of mold from one of the Finn graves and put it in his pocket. The same evening, when they came home, he strewed the mold over his father's lines unobserved. And, oddly enough, the very next time his father cast his lines, as many fish were caught as in the good old times. But after this Eilert's anxiety became indescribable. He was especially cautious while they were working of an evening round the fireside, and it was dark in the distant corners of the room. He sat there with a piece of steel in his pocket. To beg forgiveness of the dead is the only helpful means against the consequences of such deeds as his, otherwise one will be dragged off at night, by an invisible hand, to the churchyard, though one were lashed fast to the bed by a ship's hawser.

When Eilert, on the following "Preaching Sunday," went to church, he took very good care to go to the grave and beg forgiveness of the dead.

As Eilert grew older, he got to understand that the Finn folks must, after all, be pretty much the same sort of people as his own folks at home. But, on the other hand, another thought was now uppermost in his mind, the thought, namely, that the Finns must be of an inferior stock, with a taint of disgrace about them. Nevertheless, he could not very well do without Zilla's society, and they were very much together as before, especially at the time of their confirmation.

But when Eilert became a man, and mixed more with the people of the parish, he began to fancy that this old companion lowered him somewhat in the eyes of his neighbors. There was nobody who did not believe, as a matter of course, that there was something shameful about Finn blood, and he, therefore, always tried to avoid her in company.

The girl understood it all well enough, for latterly she took care to keep out of his way. Nevertheless, one day she came, as had been her wont from childhood, down to their house, and begged for leave to go in their boat when they rowed to church the next day. There were lots of strangers present from the village, and so Eilert, lest folks should think that he and she were engaged, answered mockingly, so that every one could hear him, "that church cleansing was perhaps a very good thing for Finnish sorcery," but she must find someone else to ferry her across.

After that she never spoke to him at all, but Eilert was anything but happy in consequence.

Now it happened one winter that Eilert was out all alone fishing for Greenland shark. A shark suddenly bit. The boat was small, and the fish was very big, but Eilert would not give in, and the end of the business was that his boat capsized.

All night long he lay on the top of it in the mist and a cruel sea. As now he sat there almost fainting for drowsiness, and dimly conscious that the end was not far off, and the sooner it came the better, he suddenly saw a man in seaman's clothes sitting astride the other end of the boat's bottom, and glaring savagely at him with a pair of dull reddish eyes. He was so heavy that the boat's bottom began to slowly sink down at end where he sat. Then he suddenly vanished, but it seemed to Eilert as if the sea-fog had lifted a bit; the sea had all at once grown quite calm (at least, there was now only a gentle swell), and right in front of him lay a little low gray island, toward which the boat was slowly drifting.

The skerry was wet, as if the sea had only recently been flowing over it, and on it he saw a pale girl with such lovely eyes. She wore a green kirtle and round her body a broad silver girdle with figures upon it, such as the Finns use. Her bodice was of tar-brown skin, and beneath her stay-laces, which seemed to be of green sea-grass, was a foam-white chemise, like the feathery breast of a sea bird.

When the boat came drifting onto the island, she came down to him and said, as if she knew him quite well, "So you're come at last, Eilert; I've been waiting for you so long!"

It seemed to Eilert as if an icy cold shudder ran through his body when he took the hand which helped him ashore, but it was only for the moment, and he forgot it instantly.

In the midst of the island there was an opening with a brazen flight of steps leading down to a splendid cabin. Whilst he stood there thinking things over a bit, he saw two heavy dog-fish swimming close by—they were, at least, twelve to fourteen ells long.

As they descended, the dog-fish sank down, too, each on one side of the brazen steps. Oddly enough, it looked as if the island was transparent. When the girl perceived that he was frightened, she told him that they were only two of her father's bodyguards, and shortly afterward they disappeared. She then said that she wanted to take him to her father, who was waiting for them. She added that, if he didn't find the old gentleman precisely as handsome as he might expect, he had, nevertheless, no need to be frightened, nor was he to be astonished too much at what he saw.

He now perceived that he was under water, but, for all that, there was no sign of moisture. He was on a white sandy bottom, covered with chalk-white, red, blue, and silvery-bright shells. Here were meadows of sea-grass, mountains thick with woods of bushy seaweed and sea-wrack, and the fishes darted about on every side just as the birds swarm about the rocks that sea-fowl haunt.

As they two were thus walking along together she explained many things to him. High up he saw something which looked like a black cloud with a white lining, and beneath it moved backward and forward a shape resembling a dog-fish.

"What you see there is a vessel," said she. "There's nasty weather up there now, and beneath the boat goes he who was sitting along with you on the bottom of the boat just now. If it is wrecked, it will belong to us, and then you will not be able to speak to father today." As she said this there was a wild rapacious gleam in her eyes, but it was gone again immediately.

And, in point of fact, it was no easy matter to make out the meaning of her eyes. As a rule, they were unfathomably dark with the luster of a night-billow through which the sea-fire sparkles, but occasionally, when she laughed, they took a right sea-green glitter, as when the sun shines deep down into the sea.

Now and again they passed by a boat or a vessel half-buried in the sand where fishes swam to and fro, in and out, of the cabin doors and windows. Close by the wrecks wandered human shapes which seemed to consist of nothing but blue smoke. His conductress explained to him that these were the spirits of drowned men who had not had Christian burial—one must beware of them, for dead ones of this sort are malignant. They always know when one of their own race is about to be wrecked, and at such times they howl the death warning of the Draug through the wintry nights.

Then they went further on their way right across a deep dark valley. In the rocky walls above him, he saw a row of four-cornered white doors from which a sort of glimmer, as from the northern lights, shot downward through the darkness. This valley stretched in a north eastwardly direction right under Finmark, she said, and inside the white doors dwelt the old Finn kings who had perished on the sea. Then she went and opened the nearest of these doors—here, down in the salt ocean, was the last of the kings who had capsized in the very breeze that he himself had conjured forth, but couldn't afterwards quell. There, on a block of stone, sat a wrinkled yellow Finn with running eyes and a polished dark-red crown. His large head rocked backward and forward on his withered neck, as if it were in the swirl of an ocean current. Beside him, on the same block, sat a still more shriveled and yellow little woman, who also had a crown on, and her garments were covered with all sorts of colored stones; she was stirring up a brew with a stick. If she only had fire beneath it, the girl told Eilert, she and her husband would very soon have dominion again over the salt sea, for the thing she was stirring about was magic stuff.

In the middle of a plain, which opened right before them at a turn of the road, stood a few houses together like a little town, and, a little further on, Eilert saw a church turned upside down, looking, with its long pointed tower, as if it were mirrored in the water. The girl explained to him that her father dwelt in these houses, and the church was one of the seven that stood in his realm, which extended all over Helgeland and Finnmark. No service was held in them yet, but it would be held when the drowned bishop, who sat outside in a brown study, could only hit upon the name of the Lord that was to be served, and then all Draugs would go to church. The bishop, she said, had been sitting and pondering the matter over these eight-hundred years, so he would no doubt very soon get to the bottom of it. A hundred years ago the bishop had advised them to send up one of the Draugs to Rödö church to find out all about it, but every time the word he wanted was mentioned, he couldn't catch the sound of it. In the mountain "Kunnan," King Olaf had hung a church bell of pure gold, and it is guarded by the first priest who ever came to Nordland, who stands there in a white chasuble. On the day the priest rings the bell, Kunnan will become a big stone church, to which all Nordland, both above and below the sea, will resort. But time flies, and therefore all who come down here below are asked by the bishop if they can tell him that name.

At this Eilert felt very queer indeed, and he felt queerer still when he began reflecting and found, to his horror, that he also had forgotten that name.

While he stood there in thought, the girl looked at him so anxiously. It was almost as if she wanted to help him to find it and couldn't, and with that she all at once grew deadly pale.

The Draug's house, to which they now came, was built of boat keels and large pieces of wreckage, in the interstices of which grew all sorts of seagrass and slimy green stuff. Three monstrously heavy green posts covered with shellfish formed the entrance, and the door consisted of planks which had sunk to the bottom and were full of clincher nails. In the middle of it, like a knocker, was a heavy rusty iron mooring ring with the worn-away stump of a ship's hawser hanging to it. When they came up to it, a large black arm stretched out and opened the door.

They were now in a vaulted chamber with fine shell sand on the floor. In the corners lay all sorts of ropes, yarn, and boating-gear, and among them casks and barrels and various ship's inventories. On a heap of yarn, covered by an old red-patched sail, Eilert saw the Draug, a broad-shouldered, strongly built fellow with a glazed hat shoved back onto the top of his head, with dark-red tangled hair and beard, small tearful dog-fish eyes, and a broad mouth, round which there lay for the moment a good-natured seaman's grin. The shape of his head reminded one somewhat of the big sort of seal which is called Klakkekala—his skin about the neck looked dark and shaggy, and the tops of his fingers grew together. He sat there with turned-down sea boots on, and his thick gray woolen stockings reached right up to his thigh. He wore besides, plain frieze clothes with bright glass buttons on his waistcoat. His spacious skin jacket was open, and round his neck he had a cheap red woolen scarf.

When Eilert came up, he made as if he would rise, and said good naturedly, "Good day, Eilert—you've certainly had a hard time of it today! Now you can sit down, if you like, and take a little grub. You want it, I'm sure." And with that he squirted out a jet of tobacco juice like the spouting of a whale. With one foot, which for that special purpose all at once grew extraordinarily long, he fished out of a corner, in true Nordland style, the skull of a whale to serve as a chair for Eilert, and shoved forward with his hand a long ship's drawer full of first-rate fare. There were boiled groats with syrup, cured fish, oatcakes with butter, a large stack of flatcakes, and a multitude of the best hotel dishes besides.

The Sea-Huldre bade him fall to and eat his fill, and ordered his daughter to bring out the last keg of Thronhjem *aqua vitæ.* "Of that sort the last is always the best," said he. When she came with it, Eilert thought he knew it again: it was his father's, and he himself, only a couple of days before, had bought the brandy from the wholesale dealer at Kvæford, but he didn't say anything about that now. The quid of tobacco, too, which the Draug turned somewhat impatiently in his mouth before he drank, also seemed to him wonderfully like the lead on his own line. At first it seemed to him as if he didn't quite know how to manage with the keg—his mouth was so sore, but afterward things went along smoothly enough.

So they sat for some time pretty silently, and drank glass after glass till Eilert began to think that they had had quite enough. So, when it came to his turn again, he said no, he would rather not; whereupon the Sea-Huldre put the keg to his own mouth and drained it to the very dregs. Then he stretched his long arm up to the shelf, and took down another. He was now in a better humor, and began to talk of all sorts of things. But every time he laughed, Eilert felt queer, for the Draug's mouth gaped ominously wide, and showed a greenish pointed row of teeth with a long interval between each tooth, so that they resembled a row of boat stakes.

The Sea-Huldre drained keg after keg, and with every keg he grew more communicative. With an air as if he were thinking in his own mind of something very funny, he looked at Eilert for a while and blinked his eyes. Eilert didn't like his expression at all, for it seemed to him to say: "Now, my lad, whom I have fished up so nicely, look out for a change!" But instead of that he said, "You had a rough time of it last night, Eilert, my boy, but it wouldn't have gone so hard with you if you hadn't streaked the lines with corpse-mold, and refused to take my daughter to church." Here he suddenly broke off, as if he had said too much, and to prevent himself from completing the sentence, he put the brandy-keg to his mouth once more. But the same instant Eilert caught his glance, and it was so full of deadly hatred that it sent a shiver right down his back.

When, after a long, long draught, he again took the keg from his mouth, the Sea-Huldre was again in a good humor, and told tale after tale. He stretched himself more and more heavily out on the sail, and laughed and grinned complacently at his own narrations, the humor of which was always a wreck or a drowning. From time to time Eilert felt the breath of his laughter, and it was like a cold blast. If folks would only give up their boats, he said, he had no real desire for the crews. It was driftwood and ship-timber that he was after, and he really couldn't get on without them. When his stock ran out, boat or ship he must have, and surely nobody could blame him for it, either.

With that he put the keg down empty and became somewhat more gloomy again. He began to talk about what bad times they were for him and her. It was not as it used to be, he said. He stared blankly before him for a time, as if buried in deep thought. Then he stretched himself out backward at full length, with feet extending right across the floor, and gasped so dreadfully that his upper and lower jaws resembled two boats' keels facing each other. Then he dozed right off with his neck turned toward the sail.

Then the girl again stood by Eilert's side, and bade him follow her.

They now went the same way back and again ascended up to the skerry. Then she confided to him that the reason why her father had been so bitter against him was because he had mocked her with the taunt about church-cleansing when she had wanted to go to church—the name the folks down below wanted to know might, the Sea-Huldre thought, be treasured up in Eilert's memory, but during their conversation on their way down to her father, she had perceived that he also had forgotten it. And now he must look to his life.

It would be a good deal later on in the day before the old fellow would begin inquiring about him. Till then he, Eilert, must sleep so as to have sufficient strength for his flight—she would watch over him.

The girl flung her long dark hair about him like a curtain, and it seemed to him that he knew those eyes so well. He felt as if his cheek were resting against the breast of a white sea bird, it was so warm and sleep-giving. A single reddish feather in the middle of it recalled a dark memory. Gradually he sank off into a doze, and heard her singing a lullaby, which reminded him of the swell of the billows when it ripples up and down along the beach on a fine sunny day. It was all about how they had once been playmates together, and how later on he would have nothing to say to her. Of all she sang, however, he could only recollect the last words, which were these:

> *"Oh, thousands of times have we played on the shore,*
> *and caught little fishes—dost mind it no more?*
> *We raced with the surf as it rolled at our feet,*
> *and the lurking old Sea-Huldre we always did cheat.*
>
> *"Yes, much shall thou think of at my lullaby,*
> *while the billows do rock and the breezes do sigh.*
> *Who sits now and weeps o'er thy cheeks? It is she*
> *who gave thee her soul, and whose soul lived in thee.*
>
> *"But once as an eider duck homeward I came*
> *thou didst lie 'neath a rock, with thy rifle didst aim;*
> *in my breast thou didst strike me; the blood thou dost see*
> *is the mark that I bear, oh! beloved one, of thee."*

Then it seemed to Eilert as if she sat and wept over him, and that, from time to time, a drop like a splash of sea water fell upon his cheek. He felt now that he loved her so dearly.

The next moment he again became uneasy. He fancied that right up to the skerry came a whale, which said that he, Eilert, must now make haste, and when he stood on its back he struck the shaft of an oar down its nostril, to prevent it from shooting beneath the sea again. He perceived that in this way the whale could be steered accordingly as he turned the oar to the right or left, and now they coasted the whole land of Finnmark at such a rate that the huge mountain islands shot by them like little rocks. Behind him he saw the Draug in his half-boat, and he was going so swiftly that the foam stood mid-mast high. Shortly afterward he was again lying on the skerry, and the lass smiled so blithely; she bent over him and said, "It is I, Eilert."

With that he awoke, and saw that the sunbeams were running over the wet skerry, and the Huldre-Maiden was sitting by his side. But presently the whole thing changed before his eyes. It was the sun shining through the window panes, on a bed in the Finn's hut, and by his side sat the Finn girl supporting his back, for they thought he was about to die. He had lain there delirious for six weeks, ever since the Finn had rescued him after capsizing, and this was his first moment of consciousness.

After that it seemed to him that he had never heard anything so absurd and presumptuous as the twaddle that would fix a stigma of shame or contempt on Finn blood, and the same spring he and the Finn girl Zilla were betrothed, and in the autumn they were married.

There were Finns in the bridal procession, and perhaps many said a little more about that than they need have done, but every one at the wedding agreed that the fiddler, who was also a Finn, was the best fiddler in the whole parish, and the bride the prettiest girl.

The Huldrefish

by Jonas Lie
translated by R. Nisbet Bain

It was such an odd trout that Nona hauled in at the end of his fishing line. Large and fat, red spotted and shiny, it sprawled and squirmed, with its dirty yellow belly above the water, to wriggle off the hook. And when he got it into the boat, and took it off the hook, he saw that it had only two small slits where the eyes should have been.

It must be a Huldrefish, thought one of the boatmen, for rumor had it that the lake was one of those which had a double bottom.

But Nona didn't trouble his head very much about what sort of a fish it was, so long as it was a big one. He was ravenously hungry, and bawled to them to row as rapidly as possible ashore so as to get it cooked.

He had been sitting the whole afternoon with empty lines out in the mountain lake there; but as for the trout, it was only an hour ago since it had been steering its way through the water with its rudder of a tail, and allowed itself to be fooled by a hook, and already it lay cooked red there on the dish.

But now Nona recollected about the strange eyes, and felt for them, and pricked away at its head with his fork. There was nothing but slits outside, and yet there was a sort of hard eyeball inside. The head was strangely shaped, and looked very peculiar in many respects.

He was vexed that he had not examined it more closely before it was cooked; it was not so easy now to make out what it really was. It had tasted first-rate, however, and that was something.

But at night there was, as it were, a gleam of bright water before his eyes, and he lay half-asleep, thinking of the odd fish he had pulled up.

He was in his boat again, he thought, and it seemed to him as if his hands felt the fish wriggling and sprawling for its life, and shooting its snout backward and forward to get off the hook.

All at once it grew so heavy and strong that it drew the boat after it by the line.

It went along at a frightful speed, while the lake gradually diminished, as it were, and dried up.

There was an irresistible sucking of the water in the direction the fish went, which was toward a hole at the bottom of the lake like a funnel, and right into this hole went the boat.

It glided for a long time in a sort of twilight along a subterranean river, which dashed and splashed about him. The air that met him was, at first, chilly and cellar-like; gradually, however, it grew milder, and warmer and warmer.

The stream now flowed along calmly and quietly, and broadened out continually till it fell into a large lake.

Beyond the borders of this lake, but only half-visible in the gloom, stretched swamps and morasses, where he heard sounds as of huge beasts wading and trampling. Serpent-like they rose and writhed with a crashing and splashing and snorting amidst the tepid mud and mire.

By the phosphorescent gleams he saw various fishes close to his boat, but all of them lacked eyes.

And he caught glimpses of the outlines of gigantic sea serpents stretching far away in the darkness. He now understood that it was from down here that they pop up their heads off the coast in the dog days when the sea is warm.

The lindworm, with its flat head and duck's beak, darted after fish, and crept up to the surface of the earth through the slimy ways of mire and marsh.

Through the warm and choking gloom there came, from time to time, a cooling chilling blast from the cold curves and winds of the slimy and slippery greenish lichworm, which bores its way through the earth and eats away the coffins that are rotting in the churchyards.

Horrible shapeless monsters, with streaming manes, such as are said to sometimes appear in mountain tarns, writhed and wallowed and seized their prey in the fens and marshes.

And he caught glimpses of all sorts of human-like creatures, such as fishermen and sailors meet and marvel at on the sea, and landsmen see outside the troll mounds.

And, besides that, there was a soft whizzing and an endless hovering and swarming of beings, whose shapes were nevertheless invisible to the eye of man.

Then the boat glided into miry, pulpy water, where her course tended downward, and where the earth-vault above darkened as it sank lower and lower.

All at once a blinding strip of light shot down from a bright blue slit high, high above him.

A stuffy vapor stood round about him. The water was as yellow and turbid as that which comes out of steam boilers.

And he called to mind the peculiar tepid undrinkable water which bubbles up by the side of artesian wells. It was quite hot. Up there they were boring down to a world of warm watercourses and liquid strata beneath the earth's crust.

Heat as from an oven rose up from the huge abysses and dizzying clefts, whilst mighty streaming waterfalls roared and shook the ground.

All at once he felt as if his body were breaking loose, freeing itself, and rising in the air. He had a feeling of infinite lightness, of a wondrous capability for floating in higher atmospheres and recovering equilibrium.

And, before he knew how it was, he found himself on the earth again.

ARTIST: *Laurence Housman*

The Troll on Karl Johan Square, 1892.
Henrik Ibsen, in lower-right-hand corner, seems quite undaunted by the
troll's appearance.
ARTIST: *Theodor Kittelsen*

Ibsen's Trolls:

Our Worst Selves

by Julie Jensen McDonald

Henrik Johan Ibsen (1828–1906), the great Norwegian dramatist and poet, left home at the age of sixteen to become a druggist's apprentice in the small coastal town of Grimstad.

Already dreaming of bringing truth to the stage, he soon broke away from prescriptions and found his destiny—prescribing the ideal of human striving through drama.

In *Peer Gynt*, considered by many to be his best work, the thirty-nine-year-old Ibsen gave his picturesque hero all the escapism and compromise that he condemned but could not quite bear to relinquish.

In his rigorous search for the integrated self that wills the impossible and does what it can to achieve it, Ibsen needed a repository for less worthy impulses. He projected them upon trolls, the supernatural villains Norwegians have regarded with fearful fascination since the first tale was told in the piercing cold of a northern winter.

The trolls in *Peer Gynt* have a saying, "Troll, to thyself be—enough!" This is a far cry from the idea, "Man, to thy own self be true."

To the trolls, black seems white and ugly seems fair. Peer Gynt gets into the spirit of their vision, adding, "Big seems little and dirty seems clean."

He's in dangerous company, as the trolls want to "hack him on his fingers, tug him by the hair, bite him in the haunches," and a Troll Witch asks, "Shall he be boiled into broth and bree? Shall he be roasted on a spit or be browned in a stew pan?"

The Mountain King quickly says, "There's no sense in turning recruits away. It's true he has only a single head, but my daughter, too, has no more than one. Three-headed trolls are going clean out of fashion. One hardly sees even two-headers now, and even those heads are but so-so ones."

In other words, we are so accustomed to our bad qualities that they become more human and less troll-like with the passage of time.

The oldest troll courtier asks Peer a riddle, "What is the difference between trolls and men?"

He answers, "No difference at all, as it seems to me. Big trolls would roast you and small trolls would claw you; with us it is likewise, if only we dared."

As Peer considers embracing Trolldom, he asks, "Do you want me to give up my Christian faith?"

"No," says the Mountain King, "that you are welcome to keep in peace. It's the outward cut one must tell a troll by. If we are at one in manners and dress, you may hold as your faith what to us is a horror."

So it goes in a pluralistic society. The Troll King complains that he must know himself to be real, but he has faded in the popular mind to mere legend consigned to books. Humans hold Trolldom within them, no longer so horrified by the condition that they must cast it elsewhere

Peer, still human, watches his troll bride-to-be and her sister dance and sing and sees a cow strumming a harp and a sow in socklets dancing.

The Mountain King says this can be remedied, offering to scratch and cut Peer's eyes so all that he sees "will be fine and brave," but Peer rejects the offer and flees the green-clad troll princess he came to court.

Much later, he is astonished to learn that he has begotten a troll child with the green-clad one. The mere thought of lust has engendered his surly, nasty offspring.

"Whatsoever things are lovely, whatsoever things are of good report, think on these things. As a man thinketh in his heart, so is he."

Ibsen's psychological solution to life was to contain, comprehend, and master the trolls within—a lifelong struggle of decisive battles and provisional victories.

How many of us are living as trolls and keeping it a secret, as Peer Gynt is accused of doing? Ibsen makes us ask ourselves that question. For him, enough was never enough.

A Scene from *Peer Gynt*

by Henrik Ibsen

From "Peer Gynt," by Peter Absjørnsen.
Translated by H. L. Braekstad, 1881
ARTIST: *Peter Arbo*

ACT II—SCENE VI

(The Royal Hall of the King of the Dovre Trolls. A great gathering of Trolls—Nisse, Draugen, Trollkjerring, Huldre Maidens, Fosse, etc. The King sits on his throne, scepter in hand and crown on head. His children and nearest kin sit on either side. There is great uproar and confusion in the hall.)

TROLL COURTIERS
Kill him! Kill the scoundrel
who has dared to tempt
the King's fair daughter!

TROLL CHILD
Let me chop off his fingers!

A SECOND TROLL CHILD
Let me at him! I'll rip his hair out!

HULDRE MAIDEN
I'll bite him until he's black and blue!

TROLLKJERRING (with a ladle)
I'll boil him down for our soup tonight!

A SECOND TROLLKJERRING (with a cleaver)
Toasted on a spit or boiled in a kettle, which shall it be?

TROLL KING
Silence! (motions for his counselors to approach him)
It's time for us to keep a cool head.
Matters have been going poorly for us lately,
we hardly know which way is up, and we can't
afford to turn away any assistance—no matter what
form it comes in. The lad may yet prove to be an asset!
Besides, he really doesn't look too bad,
he's very nearly blemish-free!
It's true enough that he only has one head,
but look at my daughter! She's in the same predicament!
Three-headed trolls are going out of style.
Even two-headed trolls are rarely seen nowadays,
and *their* heads aren't filled with much.
(To Peer Gynt) So, my boy, it's my daughter you desire?

PEER GYNT
Yes, if she brings with her your kingdom.

TROLL KING
You shall have half of my estate now,
and the other half when I am dead and buried.

PEER GYNT
Those terms satisfy me.

TROLL KING
But wait a minute, lad.
You've got a few pledges to make yourself;
break one of them, and our deal is off.
Then my people will skin you alive.
First of all, you must never give another thought
to the outside world—it's forever forbidden to you.
Shun the day, its deeds, and all of light's pleasures.

PEER GYNT
If I'm called King, it won't matter to me at all.

TROLL KING (rising from his throne)
Secondly—secondly we shall test your wits!
(motions for oldest counselor)

TROLL COUNSELOR
Let's see if you've got a wisdom tooth
that can crack the King's riddle-nut!

TROLL KING
What is the difference between
your kind and mine?
Tell me truly.

PEER GYNT
There isn't any, as far as I gather.
The big Trolls will crush you, the little ones claw,
it is the same with us—if only we dared.

TROLL KING
Wonderfully said! In this matter we agree,
but morning is not night and night is not morning, you see.
There's a difference between us, can you guess?
I'll tell you what it is: you Christians always say,
"Man, to thyself be true!" What rubbish! Trolls say,
"Troll, to thyself be—enough!"

TROLL COUNSELOR
Can you fathom a meaning?

PEER GYNT
You have me baffled, surely.

TROLL KING
"Enough" is a motto we hold dear,
wear it forever like a tattoo on your chest.

PEER GYNT (scratching his head)
Well, but . . .

TROLL KING
You must, if you're to be a king's successor.

PEER GYNT
Fine, so be it, if the deal comes with a wife.

TROLL KING
Next, my dear Prince Peer, you must learn
to value our simple, homely way of life.
(he motions for two trolls with pigs' heads and
white nightcaps to bring food and drink)
Our cow gives cakes and our ox gives mead;
no matter whether their taste is sweet or sour, what's
important is they're home-made and home brewed.

PEER GYNT (pushing the stuff away from him)
The devil take your home-brewed ale!
I've had enough of your country's habits.

TROLL KING
Do you see this beautiful gold drinking bowl?
He who takes the bowl gets my daughter, too.

PEER GYNT (thoughtfully)
Of course, we're taught that a man should be
master of his habits, and perhaps the drink will
not taste all that sour. Bottoms up! (drinks)

TROLL KING
Now that was sensibly said. But why do you spit?

PEER GYNT
Just a force of habit, sorry.

TROLL KING
Next you must take off all your old Christian rags;
in this mountain every Dovre Troll brags
to wear only troll-made clothes, nothing from your dale,
except, perhaps, a red silk ribbon for your tail.

PEER GYNT (disgustedly)
I haven't got a tail!

TROLL KING
No? Then you shall have one.
(to one of his attendants)
Please see that my *Royal Tail* is fastened on him.

PEER GYNT
Do you take me for a fool? I won't wear your tail!

TROLL KING
No one courts my daughter without a tail!

PEER GYNT
What! You would make a beast of a man?

TROLL KING
No, no my son, you're wrong.
I only wish to make an acceptable wooer of you.
And, as a mark of my highest esteem,
the bow you shall wear will be a bright flame color.

PEER GYNT (reflectively)
Man, after all, is but a shadow;
it's only a question of give and take.
So, tie away!

TROLL KING
Now you're coming to your senses.

TROLL ATTENDANT
Just wag and wave it, that's true troll-style!

PEER GYNT (angrily)
Now, do you have anything else you wish me to give up?
Must I also turn my back on my Christian faith?

TROLL KING
No, you are perfectly welcome to keep that.
Faith is quite free, and you pay no toll.
It's by his cut and dress that a troll is known.
We're of one mind as far as manners and costume,
you're free to believe in something we abhor.

PEER GYNT
In spite of your terms, you're really quite open-minded.
Much more reasonable than I had suspected.

TROLL KING
We trolls are better than our reputation,
my boy, and that is another of our differences.
But now the serious part of our assembly is past.
It's our eyes and our ears which shall be delighted.
Let the harp maidens awaken the Dovre Harp's strings!
Let the dancing maidens skip on the Dovre Hall's floor.
(to Peer Gynt) What do you think of it?

PEER GYNT
Think of it? Hmmm . . .

TROLL KING
Tell me openly, speak without fear.

PEER GYNT
Horrendous! Monstrous! It's really quite ugly!
An old bell-cow plucking her hoof on a harp-string,
a sow in short-stockings trying to dance to it!

TROLL COURTIERS
Eat him!

TROLL KING
He is human, he sees with Christian eyes.

HULDRE MAIDENS
Tear his eyes out, cut off his ears!

WOMAN IN GREEN (sobbing)
Must we endure his jeers
while we so prettily dance and sing?

On the Way to the Troll Castle
ARTIST: *Theodor Kittelsen*

PEER GYNT
Oh, ho! Was it you, my bride? What a surprise!
No offense was intended, it was only a joke!

WOMAN IN GREEN
You swear it was only in jest?

PEER GYNT
The dance and the music were a delight!

TROLL KING
What a queer thing, this human nature;
it clings to a man with such persistence.
If we battle it, and if it is wounded,
there may be a scar, but it heals soon enough.
My son-in-law is a most willing soul,
he has cast off his Christian clothes,
willingly drunk of the mead-filled bowl,
willingly tied on a fine troll tail!
So willingly, in fact, to do all we ask!
Who would have thought Old Adam would survive?
This calls for radical treatment,
we must find a cure for this human nature.

PEER GYNT
What do you propose to do?

TROLL KING
I'll scratch your left eye, just slightly,
then your vision will be a little off-centered.
Everything you look on will seem to be perfect.
Then I'll cut out your right-hand window.

PEER GYNT
You're drunk!

TROLL KING (laying a sharp instrument on the table)
See this glazier's tool? You must be fixed, so you'll see right.
Then you'll see how lovely your bride is,
and never again will your sight betray you
with dancing sows or bell-cows strumming.

PEER GYNT
More fool's talk!

OLD TROLL ATTENDANT
Silence! It's the Dovre King's word.
He is the wise man and you are the fool.

TROLL KING
Just think what a lot of trouble and grief
you will be rid of once and for all.
And remember, too, the eye is the source,
of the bitter, constant flood of tears.

PEER GYNT
That's true, and it says in the Good Book:
"If thine eye offend thee, pluck it out!"
How soon, my King, would my sight recover,
would it be the same as it is now?

TROLL KING
I wouldn't worry about that.

PEER GYNT
Really? Then I want no part of it.

TROLL KING
What do you mean to do?

PEER GYNT
I'm leaving.

TROLL KING
Not so fast. It's easy to get within my domain,
but the Troll Gates only swing one way.

PEER GYNT
Surely you won't keep me here by force?

TROLL KING
Come now, Peer, give way to reason!
You have a natural flair for being a troll!
You now look, act, and speak like a troll.
You want to become one truly, don't you?

PEER GYNT
Of course. I can become a Dovre Troll
if I win a bride and a kingdom of my own.
I'm not unwilling to sacrifice my pride,
but all things have a natural limit.
I have accepted a tail, with some reserve,
but I can untie the knots when I wish.
I've shed my clothes, they were old and torn,
but that won't stop me from donning them again.
And I can just as easily drop your Trollish ways.
I can easily swear that a cow's a maid,
an oath's not hard to swallow.
But to know that I can never get my freedom—
to know I won't die as a human—
to end my days as a Mountain Troll—
to never go back, so you tell me,
that's one thing that I can't endure.

TROLL KING
Now you little pip-squeak, I'm getting angry.
I'm not in the mood for your foolishness.
You scurvy worm, do you know who I am?
How dare you toy with my daughter!

PEER GYNT
You lie!

TROLL KING
You must marry her!

PEER GYNT
What are you accusing me of?

TROLL KING
Can you deny your heart's full of lust?

PEER GYNT
What the deuce does that matter?

TROLL KING
You humans will never change!
You are always ready to open your soul,
but nothing matters except what you can touch!
You think that lust doesn't matter? You'll see!
Your own eyes will show you the proof!

PEER GYNT
Unlock your gates, I'm leaving.

TROLL KING
We'll send the brat after you in a goat's skin.

PEER GYNT (mopping the sweat from his forehead)
Wake up! Wake up! This is just a dream!

TROLL KING
Shall we deliver him to your palace?

PEER GYNT
I don't care, send him wherever!

TROLL KING
As you wish, Peer, it's your decision.
What's done can't be undone, though,
and you will never see how children grow!
One day he will come looking for you.

PEER GYNT
Come on, old friend, don't act like an ass!
Fair maiden, be reasonable, let's compromise.
I must confess that I'm not rich, nor do I
have a palace. If you examine it closely,
you'll see that you've made a poor bargain.
(the woman in green faints and is carried off
 by other Huldre Maidens)

TROLL KING (with a look of contempt)
Dash him to pieces on the rocks, my children!

YOUNG TROLLS
Please, Dad, let us first play *Owls and Eagles*,
or the *Wolf Game*, or *Gray Mouse and Kitty*!

TROLL KING
Yes, but make it quick. I'm angry and tired. Good night!

PEER GYNT (chased by young trolls)
Let me go, you brats!
(tries to climb chimney)

YOUNG TROLLS
Bite him! Strike him! Punish him sorely!

PEER GYNT (trying to escape to the cellar)
Oof! Ouch!

YOUNG TROLLS
Quick, now! Plug up the holes!

TROLL ATTENDANT
How the youngsters enjoy their little games!

PEER GYNT (fighting with a troll on his back)
Let me go, you little imp!

TROLL ATTENDANT (rapping Peer's skull)
Show a little respect—he is a King's son.

PEER GYNT
A rat hole! (runs toward it)

YOUNG TROLLS
Stop up the holes! Head him off!

PEER GYNT
The old king was a scoundrel, his children are worse!

YOUNG TROLLS
Flay him!

PEER GYNT
If only I were as small as a mouse!

ARTIST: *Theodor Kittelsen*

YOUNG TROLLS
He's getting away!

PEER GYNT
If only I were as small as
a louse!

YOUNG TROLLS
Jump on his face!

PEER GYNT
(covered by a heap of trolls)
Help, Mother, I am dying!
(church bells heard in distance)

YOUNG TROLLS
Hark! The bells, the bells
in the valley!
The Black-frock's cow-bells!

(The trolls disappear,
the yelling dies away,
the palace collapses)

Viking Rune Stone with Troll Wife.
Hunstad, Scania, Denmark, Tenth
Century. The figure is that of a troll
riding on a wolf, bridled by a snake.

Grieg's Trolls

by Julie Jensen McDonald

Edvard Grieg was twenty-four when Henrik Ibsen's *Peer Gynt* was first performed in 1867, and he was inspired to compose incidental music to the playwright's lyrical fantasy about a nineteenth-century Faust.

First written as a piano duet, Grieg's composition later was orchestrated and divided into two suites (Op. 46 and 55). Among the short character pieces that make up the suite is "In the Hall of the Mountain King," Grieg's troll music.

Always trying to reflect the character and landscape of his native land, Grieg expressed the cavernous mysteries of the Troll Kingdom with hollow, minor notes—a soft quick-march that swells urgently and ends abruptly. It makes the listener feel that he or she is watching a fantastic and rather frightening scene from a safe hiding place.

The *Peer Gynt Suite* is Grieg's most popular composition, and the music also has been given credit for the perennial popularity of the play.

The Ibsen Skerry
ARTIST: *Theodor Kittelsen*

100

The Three Billy Goats Gruff

by Peter Christen Asbjørnsen and Jørgen Moe
retold by Joanne Asala

Once upon a time, and the time before that, there were three billy goats named Gruff. There was Ole Gruff, Olaf Gruff, and little Jakkob Gruff. It was springtime, and they decided to climb to the mountain meadows to munch on grass and to make themselves fat.

It wasn't an easy journey, however. To reach the high meadows, the Billy Goats Gruff had to travel through many a deep forest and cross a roaring river. There was a narrow bridge over the river, and underneath the bridge there lived a troll. He was fairly average, as far as trolls go. He was big, and ugly, and hairy, with eyes as round as saucers and teeth as sharp as knives.

"There's a troll under the bridge!" exclaimed Ole Gruff.

"Whatever shall we do?"

"Let's cross one at a time," said Olaf, "and maybe he won't notice we're here."

"I'll go," said Jakkob Gruff, the youngest of the Billy Goats Gruff. And up he trotted to the bridge.

"Cloppity, cloppity, clop!" his hooves tapped out on the wooden slats of the bridge. "Cloppity, cloppity, clop!"

A great roar sounded from beneath the bridge. "Who is that cloppity, cloppity, clopping over MY bridge?" roared the troll.

"It is I, Jakkob Gruff, the tiniest and weakest of the Billy Goats Gruff. I'm going to the mountain meadows to make myself fat."

"Ah!" called out the troll. "I'm going to gobble you right up!"

"Oh don't do that!" cried Jakkob Gruff. "I'm so small, and there is hardly any meat on my bones. Why don't you wait to gobble up my brother instead? He's ever so much bigger than I."

"Hmmm," said the troll. "That does sound like a better deal. Off you go then!"

"That wasn't so bad!" said Olaf Gruff, the middle goat. "I can do that!" And off he trotted across the bridge, cloppity, cloppity, clop!

"Who is that cloppity, cloppity, clopping across my bridge?" roared the troll.

"It is I, Olaf Gruff, middle brother of the Billy Goats Gruff. I'm going to the high meadows to sun myself, munch on grass, and make myself fat!"

"Ah, I heard you were coming," said the troll. "Wait there, I am coming up to gobble you for my supper."

"I wouldn't trouble myself if I were you," said the second Billy Goat Gruff. "I have a brother right behind me, and he's much bigger and tastier than I am!"

"Well…" the troll debated but a moment. "Okay, that sounds fair. Off you go then!"

Just then came the third Billy Goat Gruff, Ole. Cloppity, cloppity, clop! He danced across the bridge.

"Who is that making all the racket?" cried the troll.

"It is I, Ole Gruff, the biggest of the Billy Goats Gruff."

"I heard you were coming along," said the troll. "Wait there. I'll get a pinch of salt and then I'll come gobble you down!"

"Do your worst!" said Ole Gruff. "I've got two spears and I'll poke your eyes right out of your head!"

When the troll climbed to the top of the bridge, the goat charged right at him, and with his horns he Plip! Plop! Poked out each of the troll's eyes. Then he head butted the troll right off the bridge and into the river, where he never troubled anyone again.

With a toss of his head and a nod of satisfaction, the last of the Billy Goats Gruff climbed to the high mountain meadow and joined his brothers. There the three goats spent long days in the sun, munching on grass and making themselves fat for the winter.

Legends of Origin

retold by Joanne Asala

THE HULDRE FOLK

When the Lord chased Adam and Eve from the Garden of Eden, they did not have much cause for happiness. And yet, they loved each other dearly, and had many children.

One day the Lord visited Eve while she was washing her children in the river. Eve was a little ashamed that they had so many, and in her awe and wonder she hid away all those children she had not yet washed.

The Lord looked at the freshly scrubbed children, and He praised Eve because they were so beautiful. "But tell me," He said, "are all of your children here?"

"Yes, yes they are," she said.

"You don't have any others?"

"N-n-no," Eve replied shakily, "these are all the children that Adam and I have."

"I see," said the Lord, looking thoughtful. "Then let those children that you've hidden from me be hidden from man. Let those children become the Huldre Folk."

THE TROLLS

When the Lord expelled Lucifer and the other fallen angels from the Kingdom of Heaven, they fell to the earth and became the trolls. Some fell on the rooftops, and these became Nisse, who to this day live near the dwellings of men; some fell in the water, and these became the Nøkk, Fossegrimen, and Draugen. Others fell on the hills, and these became Hauge-Bokken, Risse-Gubben, and the Huldre Folk; and some fell into the mountains and became the Fjell Trollets.

There was once a widespread belief throughout Europe and Scandinavia that the Huldrer, the trolls, and other supernatural beings are descendants of either Lucifer's followers or Eve's children. Sometimes the Huldre-folk are said to be

103

descended from Adam's first wife, Lilith. Medieval theologians, by finding a place for these supernatural creatures, allowed the common people to hold onto their pagan beliefs. Protestant reformers tried to wipe out these beliefs altogether, saying that they smacked of superstition and "popery." Obviously, they were unsuccessful. But is there hope for the trolls? Perhaps.

NECKEN IS PROMISED REDEMPTION

by Sir William Alexander Craigie

In the songs which were composed in old times about Necken, he is represented, like all troll folk, as worthy of sympathy and compassion, and the country people always listen with a feeling of melancholy to the sorrowful Necken's songs, in which he laments his hard fate.

> *Oh, I am ne'er a knight, though so I seem to you,*
> *I am the wretched Necken, that dwells in billows blue,*
> *In fosses and thundering torrents.*
> *My dwelling it lies beneath a bridge so low,*
> *Where no one can walk and where no one can go,*
> *And no one can remain till the morning.*

Among the most common and most widely spread stories of Necken is the following:

A priest was one evening riding over a bridge when he heard strains of most melodious music. He turned around and saw upon the surface of the water a young man, naked to the waist, wearing a red cap, with golden locks hanging over his shoulders, and having a gold harp in his hand. He knew that it was Necken, and addressed him thus: "Why do you play your harp so merrily? Sooner shall this withered staff that I hold in my hand grow green and blossom, than you shall get redemption." The unhappy Necken threw his harp into the water, and wept bitterly.

The priest turned his horse again and rode on his way, but lo, when he had gone a little way, he noticed that round about the old pilgrim's staff that he had in his hand green shoots and leaves had come forth, mingled with the most beautiful flowers. This seemed to him to be a sign from Heaven, to preach the comforting doctrine of Redemption after another fashion, and he hastened back to the still mourning Necken, showed him the flowering staff, and said, "See, now my old staff is green, and blossoms like a rose; so also shall hope blossom in the hearts of all created beings, for their Redeemer liveth."

Comforted with this, the Necken seized his harp again, and joyous tones sounded over the banks the live-long night.

STEADY AS A ROCK

retold by Joanne Asala

There was a time in Norway when the legends of trolls were believed without question. Most of the troll legends that have come down to us are attached to certain physical structures that are supposed to be reminders of the dark days when the trolls were thought to be a real threat to the security of the villagers. Troll footprints remain in the rocks for us to see, and show what giants they really were. The strange boulders and stones that lay scattered about, particularly near churches and other holy sites, are said to have been tossed by the trolls as they tried to keep back invading Christians. The remains of trolls themselves can sometimes still be seen, for when the rays of the sun hit a troll, he would turn to stone.

THE TROLL AND THE OLD WOMAN

To the north of the village of Eithi, at the mouth of the channel that leads to the sea, there are two gigantic rocks known as *The Troll and the Old Woman*. In fair weather it is possible to take a boat between them, but in stormy seas a fisherman could be smashed against the rocks and drowned. There is a legend about these two immense landmarks, and it goes something like this:

The trolls of Iceland wanted the Faeroe Islands moved closer into their own territorial waters, and they sent out one of their own trolls and his wife to do the job of moving them.

While the troll stood in the ocean, just offshore of the Faeroe Islands, his wife climbed up the headlands and attached a stout rope around the rocks. She was to give them a nudge so the troll could carry them on his back. But the first time she tugged on the rope too hard, and the outer rocks were split off. Cursing, she tied the rope to a sturdier spot, and tugged again. The mountains would not budge. "These are not easy to move," she called out to her husband.

"Stop your whining, and let's get on with it," her husband grumbled.

"I was only making an observation, don't be snippy. I just think we should hurry."

Yet even as they spoke, they could see that the sky was beginning to turn pink. Now trolls fear daylight more than anything else, and the troll wife climbed down the headlands as quickly as she could. But they had dallied too long. As they tried to wade back through the waters to Iceland, the sun rose out of the sea, rosy and golden, and both the troll and his wife were turned to stone. There they remain to this day, looking ever outward over the seas, but unable to move.

Trolls are larger than we can imagine; they were able to wade through the deep waters surrounding Norway, and step over the tallest mountains. But sometimes in their arrogance they misjudged their own strength.

Troll Overcome by the Morning Sun, 1887
ARTIST: *Erik Werenskiold*

THE TROLL WOMAN WHO DROWNED IN THE SEA

Once a troll woman decided to wade all the way from Norway to Iceland where she wished to visit her brother. She knew that there were trenches on the ocean floor, trenches that were so deep they would cover even her head. "You shouldn't go," her friends tried to caution her. "You know that we trolls can't swim."

But the troll woman would only laugh and say, "Bah! The trenches may be deep, but I know the way, and I know I can step over them."

There was one trench, however, that was too wide for even the troll woman to step across, and she grabbed onto a passing iceberg to steady herself. But the ice was cold and slick and she lost her grip, slipping into the deep trench where she was drowned. Her body was washed up on the shores near Rauthisandur where, dead and stiffened to stone, she remains to this day.

Sometimes, the mere sound of church bells could turn a troll to stone.

THE GIANTESS'S STONE

by Sir William Alexander Craigie

Close to Kirkju-bæ in Hróars-tunga there are some remarkable cliffs, known by the name of Skersl. In these there is a cave, in which there once lived a troll-carl and a troll-carline. His name was Thorir; hers is not mentioned. These trolls drew to them every year, by sorcery, either the priest or the shepherd at Kirkju-bæ, and this went on for some time, one or other of them disappearing every year until there came a priest named Eirik. He was the most spiritual of men, and by virtue of his prayers, succeeded in defending both himself and the shepherd so well that all the attempts of the trolls were in vain. So time passed until Christmas Eve, and late on that evening the hag at last despaired of getting either the priest or the shepherd into her power. She ceased her endeavors and said to her husband, "Now I have tried till I am tired, to charm either the priest or the shepherd hither, but I cannot accomplish it, for every time that I begin my sorcery I feel as if there came against me a hot breath that is like to burn every limb and joint in my body, and so I always have to give over. Now you must go and see about some food for us, for there is nothing left to eat in the cave."

The giant was unwilling to go, but was finally persuaded by the giantess. He set off out of the cave, and held west over the ridge that has since been named after him, and called Thori's Ridge (Thoris-ás), and so out on the lake, since known as Thori's Water. Here he broke a hole in the ice, and lying down there began to fish for trout. There was a keen frost at the time, and when he thought he had caught enough and tried to rise up to go home with his catch, he found himself frozen to the ice so firmly that he could not rise at all. He struggled hard and long, but all to no purpose, and there he lay on the ice till he died.

The giantess thought her husband long in coming, and began to get hungry, so she too left the cave and went over the ridge, in the same direction as he had gone, and found him lying dead there on the ice. She tried long and hard to pull him up from it, but seeing that this could not be done, she caught up the bundle of trout and threw it on her back, saying at the same time, "This spell and charm I lay, that henceforth nothing shall be caught in this lake." Her words have taken effect, for there has been no fishing at all there ever since. She then held home to the cave, but just as she reached the brow of the ridge, it happened at one and the same moment that day broke in the east, and the church-bells sounded in her ears. She turned into stone on the top of the ridge, which has since been called Skessu-stein (The Giantess's Stone).

Shortshanks and the Ogre with Five Heads
ARTIST: *Per Krohg*

The Huldra

by Andreas Faye

Throughout the countryside there are legends about a supernatural enchantress called the Huldra, who keeps to herself in the forests and mountains. She looks just like any beautiful woman; she dresses in a white skirt and a white kerchief, but alas! she also has a cow's tail. This tail she can roll up or let hang down as she sees fit. She often seeks the company of mortals, and when she is with them she will try to conceal this tail. She especially likes to dance with handsome young men.

Once a Huldra appeared at a gathering, and everyone wanted to dance with the beautiful young girl. But while she was dancing with one of the men, he caught sight of her long tail. He realized at once what sort of creature it was that he was dancing with, but he calmed his fears and said to her "Fair maiden, you are losing your garter." She ran outdoors at once, but she later rewarded the considerate and discreet young lad with gifts of fine clothes and good cattle.

Because the Huldra can change herself into the most beautiful of maidens, and promise the lads the moon, she is incredibly dangerous, far more dangerous to men than the Huldrer men are to young virgins. Whoever has relations with a Huldra girl will find it difficult to get rid of her again. She is with him constantly. Whenever he turns around, she is there. Sometimes a Huldra will fall in love with a lad, and will let herself be christened and married. During one of these ceremonies, her long cow-tail usually falls off. But if the man is not agreeable, and if the Huldra tries to take him away, he need only say the name of our Savior and neither the Huldra nor any other creature can have power over him. Occasionally a man will be lured into the mountain, and afterwards he is never quite the same again.

Huldre Legends

by William Alexander Craigie

THE WOOD HULDRE

"In my young days," said a woodcutter, "I saw the Wood-Huldre with my own eyes; she had a red knitted jacket, a green bodice, and blue gown. She ran past me with her long yellow hair flying loose about her; she was pretty in the face, but behind she was as hollow as a baking-trough. A thick vapor can sometimes be seen rising from the flat rocks, and one knows that she is boiling her clothes; and often during thunder loud noises can be heard coming from them, as if a whole load of stones were emptied down. This is her beating her clothes. She can sometimes be seen with a child on her arm; my own father saw this, and had heard that she had a husband, although she is given to enticing men to her. It is not easy to find out the husband's proper name, for some say that she is in the habit of calling on Erik, while others think that she and the 'hornufve' are a couple.

"Many years ago, it happened that a man, who was burning charcoal in the thick forest, was several times visited by a Wood-Huldre, who wished to warm herself at his fire. He was annoyed at this, and threw a burning coal at her. Then she screamed, 'Ture Koppar-bonde, the man took red hot and burned me.' Others say that she screamed, 'Svante, Svante, the man burned me.' He was then heard saying, 'Self answer and self have!' But whatever his name was, and whatever answer he gave, a terrible noise was heard in the forest, so that the coal-burner took to his heels, and ran away as fast as he could, and so escaped the danger.

"I know a man myself, who saw her sitting, combing her hair; he was wrong in the head for a long time after that sight. It might, however, have been worse for another man that I heard tell of. He had gone out to look for his master's cows, and searched for them till late in the evening. By this time he had gone astray, and had found no cows. He then saw a light at some distance further into the forest, and went toward it, in the belief that some human beings lived there. There was a house, sure enough, and the door was open, so he entered and bade them good evening. At the end of the table, with her back against the wall, sat a woman, whom he took to be the good wife, and asked her whether he could stay there overnight. 'That may well be,' said she, 'you can lie in the bed that is made up in the room there.' He thanked her, and began to undress, and in doing so happened to throw his clasp-knife on the coverlet. He then thought he heard a splash, as if the knife had fallen into water, but tired as he was, he sat down on the bed, saying, 'So, in Jesus' name, now I have gone enough today.' As he said this, he sank into a pool, so that the water splashed up over him. At the same instant the house, and everything in it, had disappeared, and the man found himself sitting in a pool of water in the forest while his clothes were hanging on a bush beside him. He could thank the name he had named, that he escaped as he did; for had he lain down in the Wood-Huldre's bed and her husband would soon have come and torn him to pieces.

"A generation ago, it happened in Stene-stad that a peasant, who was out in the forest in broad daylight, looking to his cattle, found a lamb lying by itself beside a bush. He took it up gently, and carried it home to his house where his wife petted it all she could, and let it lie under the stove.

From "The Coal Burner and the Troll" by Herman Hofberg, 1895
ARTIST: *Unknown*

112

"Later in the day the man again went out to the forest, and heard a piteous voice, which said, 'My child! My child! Where is my child?' The man could see no one, and went home again. There he told what he had heard, and wondered who it could be that was crying in this way for the child. 'That was my mother,' cried the lamb, and made out at the door, across the yard and into the forest. They knew then that this was the Wood Huldre's child, which she had changed into the shape of a lamb, and which they had taken care of. As thanks for this they had great luck with their cattle, which were always much finer than their neighbors'."

THE PEASANT AND THE WOOD HULDRE

There was once a peasant who was always equally cool and collected, whether things went with him or against him, so that no one was ever able to startle him, or make him either laugh or cry. They might say what they pleased; he had always his answer ready, and had the last word with them. He had been at work in the woods all week, and was going home on Saturday evening, when he met a Huldre maiden who tried to get the better of him.

"I have been at your house," said she.
"Then you weren't at home that time," said he.
"Your wife has had a child," said she.
"It was her time then," said he.
"She has got twins," said she.
"Two birds in one egg," said he.
"One of them is dead," said she.
"That's only one coffin then," said he.
"Your wife is dead as well," said she.
"Saves her crying for the children," said he.
"Your house is burned down," said she.
"When the tail's seen, the troll's known," said he.
"If I had you out at sea," said she.
"With a ship under me," said he.
"With a hole in it," said she.
"And a plug in that," said he.

THE HULDRE DANCE

The thicket at Havers-lund was full of Huldre Maidens, and in the village lived a man who had a good-looking son named Tammes. The Huldrer had a loving eye for him, and he often heard their song and music, and watched their dance when he drove the cattle down to the fold late in the evening. He often stayed away for a long time, and then his father scolded him, but his longing only grew all the greater. Finally, late one evening, he ventured so near that they formed a circle round him, and he came home no more. For three years his parents waited for him in vain. Then they heard tell of a wise woman, who was said to be able to help them, so they got her down there one evening, and waited outside the thicket with anxious attention. Finally the dance stopped, and the Huldrer disappeared, leaving something lying on the ground. It was Tammes, but he was dead. They had danced him to death, and the blood was flowing from his nose and mouth. After this nothing succeeded with Nis Tamsen, whereas everything had gone well with him while his son was with the Huldrer. This happened in the year 1700.

The Huldre Bridegroom

retold by Joanne Asala

One summer, many, many years ago, the young people took the cattle up to the *sæter* near Melbustad, in Hadeland, for their summer grazing. But they had only been there about a week before the cows grew restless, temperamental and nearly impossible to keep under control. The village girls took turns trying to herd them, but the situation did not improve until a certain girl, recently engaged, came to work with them. The cows grew immediately quiet in her presence, and followed her around like little lost lambs. They were no longer difficult to manage. She lived in the *sæter* all alone, with only her dog for company. The others thought that the calming effect she had was very strange, but since the girl had always been so sweet and innocent, they did not suspect witchcraft.

Late one afternoon, as she was sitting in her rocker, her sweetheart came in and sat down in the chair beside her. "I have decided I cannot wait any longer," he said. "I want to get married right away."

The girl sat quite still and did not say a word. There was something about the unexpected visit that made her feel very uneasy.

The young man seemed to read the question in her eyes, "No, I haven't lost my mind, I just want to be wed to you now instead of later. Let's get married immediately."

In twos and threes people began to file into the *sæter*, and they set the table with fine silver and china, and brought out dishes of every description. The bridesmaids carried in a beautiful crown and a wedding gown of the softest fabric, which they dressed her in. They placed the crown on her head and put rings on her fingers. But still the girl did not say a word.

The people were all people she knew, women from the farms and girls she grew up with. But the girl noticed that her dog seemed uneasy. He sat under the table growling low in his throat. Then he bolted out the door and ran straight down the path to Melbustad, whining and barking all the way.

The dog carried on so that the boy who was really the girl's sweetheart took down his rifle and followed the dog back to the *sæter*. When he came to the yard, he saw that it was filled with saddled horses, and finer horses he had never seen. He crept over to the little cottage and peeked in through the window. Because he did not fall under the same enchantment as his betrothed, it was easy for him to see that the room was filled with trolls and other Huldre folk. He took his gun and fired it over the door of the cottage. At that very moment the door burst open, and one ball of gray wool after another came tumbling over the threshold, each one bigger and smellier than the last. Then there was silence. The boy stepped into the cabin and saw his sweetheart dressed as a bride. He had come just in the nick of time.

"For St. Peter's sake!" he exploded. "What is going on here?" He glanced around the room, now decorated with wilted branches and flowers, and he saw the silver on the table. But all of the rich delicacies had transformed into moss and toadstools, cow dung and toads, and other such creepy, crawling, slimy things. It made him queasy to think of eating them.

"What's going on?!" asked the girl indignantly. "As if you didn't know! You've talked about nothing but our wedding all day!"

"No, I just came in now," he said. "It must have been one of the trolls who made himself look like me." The girl looked so bewildered that her sweetheart knew she was still partly under the trolls' spell. He took her hand and led her back down to the village so that nothing more could happen to her, and when they got there he married her on the spot, as she was dressed in the Huldre finery. Never again was the girl bothered by the Huldre folk, and her crown and the wedding gown were hung in the church at Melbustad, where they are said to be to this very day.

The Spirit of the Farm

by Joanne Asala

The protection of the farm and the welfare of its inhabitants were the responsibility of the Nisse, also known as the Tunkall, the Tomte, the Tuftebonde, the Tuftekall, the Gobonde, the Gardsbonde, the Tunvord, the Gardvord, and the Tusse, depending on what part of Norway you were from. The Nisse keeps all evil powers away from the farm, and even the Oskorei, the Host of Midnight Riders, will keep their distance if a Nisse is present.

The name "Nisse" is very old and is said to derive from the Scandinavian form of Nicholas. The Nisse lives in the farmer's barn and keeps watch over the livestock. The farm that is lucky enough to have a Nisse will have healthy, well-groomed animals, especially horses. The mysterious plaits found in the horse's tail are called Nisse-plaits, and it is unlucky to undo them.

The Nisse lives alone and has neither wife nor children; but he seems to be a congenial sort unless matters are not going his way. Then he is a terror.

NO BUTTER ON THE PORRIDGE

One Christmas Eve, so far back that no one can say for sure when, a servant girl wanted to tease the family Nisse by playing a little trick on him. She hid the butter at the bottom of the Rømmegrøt, instead of placing it on top, and set the porridge bowl out in the barn. She knew how much the Nisse loved his butter, and she couldn't wait to get a look at his face when he discovered there was none.

But she got more than she expected! When the Nisse saw that there was no butter on his Christmas porridge, he flew into a rage. He immediately went to the cow shed and killed the best cow, even though he had cared for it tenderly all year. "No, butter, eh?" he thought spitefully. "That will make them sit up and take notice! How dare they be so stingy as to deny me a little butter!"

However, he ate the porridge anyway. And there, in the bottom of the bowl, he discovered the butter. How terrible he felt about killing the prize cow! How he cried and wailed!

That same Christmas Eve, the Nisse crept over to a farm in the next village, and took the best cow he could find, although it did not look half so fine as the one he had tended. But give him time.

So the Nisse can be a helpful friend, but a dangerous enemy to cross. It does not cost much to feed him, in view of how much work he does, and so it is better to remember the courtesy of giving him his butter. But perhaps you have noticed that, despite his good qualities, the Nisse is also a thief.

The Nisse, 1887
ARTIST: *Theodor Kittelsen*

THE STOLEN FODDER

Near Hjartdal there lived a farmer who was quite well off, and who seemed to his neighbors to have the strangest good fortune with his cattle. No matter how many cows he had, they all seemed full and sleek.

But one hard winter even he ran out of feed, and he became terribly worried. One day he was talking to his wife about their troubles, when he heard a voice call down the chimney, "I will help you."

He and his wife exchanged looks of confusion, but they decided to do nothing and wait to see what would happen, and to their amazement, although there was no fodder in the grain storage, the cows seemed content and happy.

"I'm going to risk the deep snows and go to town to buy some fodder," the man said to his wife. "I'm not sure why our cows look so healthy, but I don't trust it to last forever." He had only gone halfway when he discovered a huge drift of snow blocking the road.

"Do not worry," said a voice. "Go home. I will help you."

And so the farmer went home. Time passed, and while he never saw any fodder in the bins, the cows continued to look fat and well-groomed.

"I can't stand not knowing what is happening to my cattle, I must see what is going on," said the farmer to his wife, and that night he crept into the barn and waited in the shadows. It was not long before a Nisse entered his barn, dragging along behind him a tiny bundle of hay. It was quite a burden for him; he was sweating and puffing and looked near about to collapse.

The man thought this was terribly funny, and he said in a sarcastic voice, "Well, that hardly looks like it should be an effort."

The Nisse turned nearly as red as his jacket, and he shouted, "You'll regret this day, for now I'm going to steal from you as much as I've stolen for you! Let's see how you like that!" It didn't take long before the man's cows began to disappear, one by one, and it didn't take long for the remaining cows to starve to death.

Besides being a hard worker and a thief, the Nisse is also a prankster. He'll trip people in the dark, pinch the milkmaid, tie knots in your hair and put out the hearth fire. Can you get rid of a Nisse? Just try!

THE BOTHERSOME NISSE

There was a small farm in Rogaland where the Nisse was impossible to live with. The farmer tried everything possible to get rid of him, but without any luck. The only solution he saw left to him was to sell the place and move on. Finally, he had nearly everything moved to the new farm except for a last load of miscellaneous boxes and barrels, all of which were supposedly empty. But one of these "empty" barrels was quite heavy to lift, and when he pulled off the lid, the little bearded face of the Nisse grinned up at him. "Moving Day!" he laughed.

Dobbin and the Goblin, 1905
ARTIST: *Theodor Kittelsen*

Water Trolls

A Collection of Legends and Stories

The artist Theodor Kittelsen knew the trolls of Norway quite well, and his trolls are considered by many to be the only genuine trolls. Of all the artists who have created illustrations of these mythical creatures, his are the most famous. He was also a masterful storyteller. No one has ever been able to capture the wild, untamed Norwegian landscapes of the trolls in quite the same way.

NØKKEN

by Theodor Kittelsen
translated by Joanne Asala

Nøkken is a sly creature, and he is a hunter of humans. When the sun sets, you would be wise to beware. He may be hiding beneath that large, spreading water lily you are trying to reach out to. No sooner have you touched it than the quagmire pulls you down—and he clutches you in his wet, slimy hands.

Or perhaps as you sit alone by the lake in the evening, memories will rise to the surface, first one, then another, then in droves, memories with the same warm hue and brilliance as the rays that reflect among the leaves and lilies. Oh, be especially on your guard then! These are the feelings on which Nøkken plays. The waters call up memories, and Nøkken lies there—lurking below. He grins because he knows how easily we are ensnared by that beautiful, rippling reflection.

Nøkken may appear in any number of disguises. Sometimes he will lie on the beach as some bright, shining gemstone—touch it and you are in his power. He is so cunning that he can lie there in the form of a forgotten fishing rod, with both line and hook attached.

There is another old trick that he has used so many times that hardly anyone will fall for it anymore. He disguises himself as a small skiff, half drawn up on shore. Still it happens that some foolish person will come along, see the boat and think, "My! What a wretched wreck of a boat. It is half-filled with water! But say, there is an old tin bucket! I wonder...." He bails out the boat, then shoves out into the water.

At first all is well, for Nøkken likes to toy with his victim like a cat plays with a mouse. How wonderful it is to glide among the lilies! The lake is so calm and so still. A short distance away lies a tiny island with a birch tree on it. What fun it would be to row over there!

But in the middle of the lake the old skiff begins to leak. The bottom cracks and the boat sinks. Then the Nøkken throws off his disguise, and drags his prey down into the dark depths.

Sometimes Nøkken appears as a gray horse, grazing contentedly near the lake. He hopes to lure some fool onto his back, and then he will gallop straight into the water with him.

Once upon a time there was a farmer who came across the gray horse. It was sleek and shiny and the farmer thought that here was an excellent animal, indeed. But for the life of him, he could not imagine what such a fine creature would be doing there. Scratching his head, he finally decided to go home and get a halter, and he hid it carefully under his jacket. The horse was still nibbling on the grass when he returned.

Nøkken
ARTIST: *Theodor Kittelsen*

"Here, horsey! Come here, fellow, come on," urged the man, and the horse came. His only thought was how to get the farmer to mount him.

But all of a sudden the farmer grabbed the horse by the nostrils, and then there was a change in the drama! Nøkken kicked and bucked, but it was to no avail. The halter was on in an instant, and the farmer gave him a friendly slap on his fat rump. "Now, my pretty, you'll come with me!"

Nøkken was in his power, but was far from pleased at being locked in the smelly, stuffy stable. He was accustomed to lying in the fresh lake waters and peeping out from among the water lilies. Nor was he any happier when he got outside, for the farmer used him to plow all of his fields. And plow he did! He had the strength of twenty horses, and the dirt clods flew!

"That horse is worth his weight in gold," thought the farmer. "He works like the devil himself." Yet sometimes the wild eyes, which stared at him so strangely, caused him to shudder. When the sun set, the gray horse became so wild and mad that it was impossible for anyone to be in the barn with him. He neighed and shrieked the whole night long, and kicked and dug so that the splinters flew.

Nøkken as a Horse, 1907
ARTIST: *Theodor Kittelsen*

At first the farmer found it all terribly amusing, but slowly a shadow of unease settled over him. He found no peace. It was as if a band was tightening around his neck, and he gave a start. He thought he saw ribbons of light reflecting in the deep, black water. He himself lay sinking deeper and deeper in the bottomless muck and mire.

"I'll give you a ten dollar gold piece, Ola, if you take the halter off the gray horse!" he said to his farmhand.

"Heck, I'd do that for a dollar," Ola replied. When the halter came off, the gray horse didn't hesitate for a second, he bolted right through the wall so that the wooden beams crashed like match sticks.

Old Inger Bakken, who lived near the lake, said afterward that the gray horse came galloping right through his potato patch. "Smoke poured from his nostrils and his tail was up in the air like the horn of an old ram!" she said. "And how he flew by! Lord help me if he didn't plunge right into that water so that the spray rose like a wall all around him!"

Kittelsen not only had knowledge of Nøkken, but of the Fossegrim as well.

THE FOSSEGRIM

by Theodor Kittelsen
translated by Joanne Asala

Sit down by the plunging waters of the falls, at the next full moon, and if you are lucky you may both see and hear the Fossegrim.

Behind the lacy curtain, in the cauldron of foam, he sits and plays tunes that have been around since the beginning of time. At first it only sounds like the crashing din of water, but slowly you become mesmerized by the melodies, and it will be all you can do to keep from throwing yourself in the churning waters.

The sound of thunder comes from his bow, and the sweet notes speak of mountainous crags and silent forests. All the powers of nature vibrate in the strings, and the pealing echoes fill the night as the song rises in one magnificent chord.

The fir trees sigh, the aspens quake; the streams murmur, and the birches tremble. Shouts of pure joy come from the winds off the mountains. The forest's stillness is like a sigh, and the quiet forest lake sings all the gentle melancholy tunes of the willow flute. Fossegrim bends dreamily over his fiddle, his bow flies back and forth in great, moving strokes—everything must come forward, out, over the fall and into the tumult below.

He plays with eyes shut, looks upon himself with his inner eye, is himself in the middle of the wild water. See how he taps his foot in time! His music is like eternity. The great mountains rise up into a mighty temple in which can dwell his everlasting music. High up in the dark blue vault of the heavens hangs the silvery moon, mirroring herself in the waves of the deep pools.

Star upon star twinkles in the darkness. The music grows wilder. It is as if every note would become part of the myriad, would spread out, sparkling among the rest. The fiddler sits with his eyes closed, his head bent over his violin. It is his music that binds him to the watery deep.

Sometimes the Fossegrim is mistaken for the Kvernknurr, a different troll entirely, but one also associated with water—particularly water mills.

THE TROLL AT THE MILL

retold by Joanne Asala

One cold and dark winter night a farmer was grinding at the mill in Flesberg, although no one was supposed to stay there or let the mill grind anything after dark, for the Kvernknurr hated to be disturbed and had an awful temper. Perhaps the man didn't really believe this, perhaps he didn't care, but the fact remains that he was there at a time that everyone had warned him not to be.

Just as he was getting ready to leave, he heard a terrible pounding on the walls, BANG! Then it came from the floor beneath his feet, BANG! Suddenly, BANG! The door flew open and slammed into the wall, and there in the doorway was a skull, gleaming white in the moonlight and filling the entire entrance. The chin was on the threshold, the forehead reached the top of the frame, and the cheekbones stretched from side to side. Then the skull began to shriek, a terrible, scratchy voice that made the hair on the farmer's neck rise.

Luckily the troll was too big to fit through the doorway, and as long as the farmer stayed where he was, he thought he would be safe. But a long, hairy, clawed hand snaked inside and grasped the farmer in a fist. He was pulled out into the night, and held up before the gaping mouth of the skull. A foul breath issued from the troll's mouth as he shouted, "I'll let you go this time, without a mark, but don't ever come back here after it's dark! You can bet that the next time your bones I will break to be a reminder to all that you kept me awake!" Without another word he tossed the farmer head-first into a snowbank.

Not all water trolls lived near streams or rivers. Some lived in the wide expanses of lakes and oceans. Only the very bravest of souls would dare travel on the water alone.

THE TROLL OF THE LAKE

retold by Joanne Asala

My grandfather's grandfather, whose name was Eirik, lived in the North Country, and he was very poor. But though he was poor, everyone loved him for the kindness he showed to others.

One Christmas Eve, late in the night, he crossed over the frozen lake to beg for some food to feed to his children the next day. The farmer gladly gave him a smoked piece of mutton and Eirik, vowing to chop wood in exchange for the meat, returned happily homeward.

When he reached the middle of the lake, he heard a terrible creaking noise behind him. He spun around, but saw nothing. The moon reflected brightly on the smooth, unbroken ice, and all seemed still. Uneasy, Eirik traveled a few more yards when all of a sudden he saw the ice beneath his feet begin to crack. He ran ahead, and just in time, too, for a monster broke through the ice and towered above him.

The monster was horrible to behold, with six heads and foul-smelling breath. This troll ran after Eirik, who saw no chance to escape with the meat, so he dropped the side of mutton and ran for shore as fast as his legs could carry him.

The next morning he went out again onto the frozen lake to see if there might be anything left of his mutton. But look as he did, all he found were the scattered remains of cracked and gnawed bones.

The Troll Washing His Brat
ARTIST: *Theodor Kittelsen*

The Troll Changelings

by Joanne Asala

The belief in changelings probably arose from the desire of parents to have healthy, normal children. Today, parents usually accept the fact when their child has a physical or mental retardation, but our ancestors did not. Handicapped and critically ill children were often not accepted by their parents, and were either abused or neglected. Some parents believed that their own child had been kidnapped by trolls and replaced with a baby not their own—a troll changeling.

The reasons for this kidnapping were varied. Perhaps it was to bring a new strain of blood into the troll race, or an opportunity to get rid of one of their own sickly troll children.

Every pregnant woman was afraid that her child would be taken away. The mother knew that the trolls were watching her with interest, waiting to make the switch, so she took all necessary precautions. The christening of a baby would protect it, and so babies were brought to the church as quickly as possible after birth. The child was never left alone; at night a candle was kept burning and a watch was set. The baby was never taken outside until the day of the christening, and even then was protected by something made of steel—a pin or a knife. There were other charms as well—a prayer book, a sacramental host, a cross. But sometimes children were taken anyway.

THE UNBAPTIZED CHILD

Once, in a home where a child was just born, the mother fell asleep with the baby in her arms. The midwife and the other women fell asleep in their chairs because they had all been awake for a long time.

The mother was not sleeping soundly, and woke to feel something moving on the bed. To her shock she discovered that her baby was gone, and in its place was a shriveled troll child. Looking around, she saw a troll hag sitting on the window sill, holding the babe in her arms. She was trying to climb out, but it was a high window and she was having trouble.

"My baby!" The mother let out an agonized scream and shouted, "May Jesus, Mary and Joseph protect my child!"

The troll hag dropped the baby and scrambled out the window. The troll child vanished. The mother, though still weak from her ordeal, jumped out of bed to scoop up the child. The midwife did not hesitate for a moment. She fetched the minister, and the child was baptized right away.

Sometimes the means of ridding oneself of a troll child were a little more severe than calling out the Lord's name.

BURNING THE CHANGELING

In the town of Vang, in Oppland, there was a changeling who would not speak.

One day the dairy maid got up very early to do the milking, and she heard a voice shout from behind the stable, "Come on, Ping!"

The girl ran to the house and told everyone what had happened, and the changeling exclaimed, "Why, that's my mother!"

The parents were terribly surprised to hear the baby speak, and the mother said, "She's your mother? Carl! Fire up the oven!"

Her husband fired up the oven, and picked up the troll child, making as if he were going to pitch it into the flames head first.

"Stop!" a voice screeched from the door.

Everyone spun around to see a troll hag standing in the doorway. She held a healthy looking human child in her arms. "I have never treated your child the way you are treating mine!"

Then she snatched her own child and disappeared.

In "The Wise Woman," Peter Christian Asbjørnsen tells us about another changeling.

THE WISE WOMAN

by Peter Christian Asbjørnsen

My great-grandmother used to live in Joramo, in Lesja, and the story goes that she had a changeling. I, of course, never saw him for she was dead and he was gone long before I was ever born. But my father told me about him. He had the leathery face of an old man; he had eyes as red as a carp's, and they glowed in the dark like an owl's. His head was as long and thin as a horse's, and as big around as a cabbage. He had legs as hairy as a sheep's, and a body as bony as a starved chicken's. All he ever did was whine and cry and howl and yell, and whenever he got a grasp of something, he would throw it straight at my great-grandmother's head. He was always ravenous with hunger, and would eat anything he saw. He practically ate them out of house and home! The older he got, the surlier he grew, and there was never a rest from his constant screeching. But for all his noise he never said a word.

He was the nastiest troll child that anyone had ever encountered, and they did not know what to do. His parents sought advice from everyone they met, and they were told to do first one thing, and then another. The most common advice was to beat the troll brat, but the mother didn't really have the heart to thrash him until she knew for certain that he was a changeling.

My grandmother's sister stopped by one day and said, "You should look out your window and say that you see the king coming, and then light a big fire on the hearth and break an egg. Hang the shell over the fire, and put the measuring rod down through the chimney pipe."

Well, the mother did this, and the child was silent and watchful. He stood up in his cradle and stared. Then he stretched his body, stretched it so that his legs were still in the crib but his head was peeking into the fire pit—stretched all the way across the room.

"Old I am now, that I've seen the Forest of Lesja burn down and grow up seven times again, but never before have I seen such a big porridge stirrer in such a tiny cauldron!"

When the mother heard this, she knew she had heard enough. This was indeed a changeling, and she started to abuse him, and one Thursday evening even took him onto the garbage heap and gave him a real thrashing. Then there was a whimpering and a crying around her. The second Thursday she did the same, and she heard the crying from the woods again, and this time she heard someone speak as if beside her, and she could tell that it was the voice of her own child.

"Every time you beat Tjøstul Gautstigen, they beat me inside Troll Mountain."

But on the next Thursday evening, she gave the troll child another beating. Then an old troll hag came flying up with a human child, as quick as summer lightning. "Give me Tjøstul, and you can have your brat back!" she said, and tossed the child at its mother.

The Noisy Neighbors*

retold by Joanne Asala

One day a Fjell-Troll shouted from atop his mountain, "I hear a cow bellowing from the valley!"

Seven years later a Jøtul shouted in reply, "Couldn't it just as well be the roar of the ocean's waves?"

Another seven years passed before a Draug poked his head from beneath the waves and screamed, "Will you shut up! With all this yammering I can hardly hear myself think!"

The Sea Troll, 1887
ARTIST: *Theodor Kittelsen*

---

*Throughout Norwegian legend, trolls were depicted as stupid, slow to react, and easy to trick.

The Twelve Wild Ducks

retold by Joanne Asala

Once on a time, in the middle of winter, there was a beautiful queen who was out riding in her sleigh. There had been a new fall of snow, and the day was crisp and clear. She sat sewing near her window, and as she sewed the sleigh hit a bump in the road and she pricked her finger with her needle. She called for the driver to stop and stepped outside of her carriage. And so, as she stood leaning against the ebony door, she saw how the red blood looked so pretty on the white snow, and she fell to thinking how she had twelve sons and no daughters. She said to herself, "If only I had a daughter as white as snow and as red as blood and as dark as ebony, I shouldn't care what became of all my sons."

The words were scarce out of her mouth when the old witch of the Troll People came out of the woods. "I heard what you said, and if it's a daughter you want, it's a daughter you shall have, and she shall be as white as snow and as red as blood and as dark as ebony. In return your twelve sons shall be mine. Although," she added, "you may keep them until the babe is christened."

So when the time came, the queen had a daughter, and she was all that she had wished for; she was as white as snow and as red as blood and as dark as ebony—just as the troll witch had promised. They named her the Dark Rose of Winter, but called her Snow White for her fair complexion. Well, there was great joy at the king's court, you can be sure, and the queen was as glad as glad could be. But when she remembered the promise she had made, she knew she could not give up her sons. She called for the silversmith and asked him to make a silver spoon for each of her sons to carry in his pocket, and one more for her new daughter Snow White. The queen had heard that metal was a charm against faeries, and she hoped that the spoons would keep the troll witch away.

Yet despite all of the queen's careful planning, at the very moment the princess was christened, her twelve brothers were turned into twelve wild ducks, and they flew out of the church and into the sky. They were never seen again; away they had flown and away they stayed. The queen had been foolish to think that silver would stop the troll witch. Trolls were well-known for their metal-working skills.

Time passed and the princess grew up. She was tall and had long dark hair. She was kind and generous, beautiful and merry, and everyone who met her could not help but love her. But there were also times when she was strange and sad, and no one could understand what it was that failed her.

One evening the queen, too, was sorrowful, as she often was when she thought of her sons, and she asked her daughter, "Why are you so sad, my darling? Is there anything you want? If so, you need only tell me, and you shall have it."

"It's so quiet around here," Snow White complained. "It's so dull and lonely, everyone else has brothers and sisters, but I am alone. I have nobody, and that's why I'm sad."

"But you had brothers, my daughter," said the queen. "I had twelve sons who were your brothers, but I gave them all away to get you." And so she told her the whole story.

When Snow White heard the dreadful story of her birth, she had no rest; for in spite of all the queen could say or do, and all she wept and prayed, the girl insisted she would set off to seek her brothers. She thought that their enchantment was all her fault.

One day she was finally able to sneak away from the palace. On and on she walked into the wide world, much farther than she had ever gone before, farther than anyone in the kingdom had ever traveled. When she was walking through a great, great woods, she suddenly felt very tired, and she sat down on a mossy tuft and was soon fast asleep. In her dream she went deeper into the woods, till she came to a little wooden hut, and there she found all twelve of her brothers. But before she could speak to them, she woke up. In front of her, where she could have sworn there was nothing before, she now saw a well-worn path that cut through the moss. The path led deeper into the woods, and since that was where the dream said her brothers were, she followed it. After awhile she came to the little wooden hut she had seen in her dream.

Now, when she went into the room there was no one at home, but there stood twelve beds, and twelve chairs, and twelve spoons—a dozen of everything! When Snow White saw all of this, she was very happy. In fact, she had never felt this happy before. It was obvious that her brothers lived here, and that they owned the twelve beds and chairs and spoons. But what a mess it all was, and cold! She made a fire, and then swept the room, and made the beds and cooked up a fine dinner. She tried to make the house as tidy as she could, and when she had done all the cooking and work, she ate her own dinner and crept under her youngest brother's bed, and lay down there. Then she remembered that she had left her silver spoon on the table.

She had scarcely laid herself down before she heard something flapping and whirring in the air, and suddenly twelve ducks came swooping into the yard. Yet as soon as they crossed the threshold into the hut, they turned into men.

"Oh, how nice and warm it is in here," they said to one another, "heaven bless him who made up the fire and cooked such a fine dinner for us."

Each of the twelve brothers took from the table his silver spoon and was about to eat when the youngest of them spoke up, "Say, each of us has our own spoon, and yet there is one still lying on the table."

"You're right," said the oldest, "and it looks just like the ones we all have."

"This must be our sister's spoon," spoke another of them. "And if her spoon is here, she can't be very far off herself!"

Snow White was about to crawl out from under the bed when she heard the fourth of her brothers speak, "If this is our sister's spoon, and she is here, she shall be killed. She is to blame for all we've suffered."

"No," said a fifth, "that would not be right. It would be a shame to kill her for that. She has nothing to do with any of our suffering or ill. If anyone's to blame, it's our own mother."

They immediately set to work hunting for her both high and low, and Snow White shivered under the bed. But it was a small hut, and she could not hide forever. The brothers searched under each of the beds, and when they came to the youngest prince's bed, they found her, and dragged her out. The one brother still wanted her killed, but she begged and begged that they would not.

"Oh, please, don't kill me! I've been searching for you all for three years, and our parents have no idea where I am. I've come to set you free, if I can."

"There is a way to save us," said the sixth of the brothers.

"What is that?" Snow White asked.

The seventh spoke up, "You must pick thistledown, and you must card it, and spin it, and weave it; and after you have done that, you must cut out and make twelve coats and twelve shirts and twelve neckerchiefs, one for each of us, and while you do that, you must neither talk, nor laugh, nor weep. If you can do that, we are free."

Snow White could not believe her ears, "I am to sew you new clothes? Is this a joke? Isn't it enough that I cleaned this pigsty you call a home?"

"I know it is a strange request," said the eighth brother, "but that is what the troll witch demanded be done before she would set us free."

The Twelve Wild Ducks, 1907
ARTIST: *Theodor Kittelsen*

"But wherever shall I find enough thistledown to make so many outfits?" Snow White asked.

"We'll show you," said the ninth brother. And so they took her with them to a great, wide moor where there stood such a crop of thistles, all nodding and nodding in the breeze, and the down all floating and glistening like gossamers through the air in the sunbeams. Snow White had never seen such a quantity of thistledown in her life, and she began to pluck and gather it as fast as she could. Her brothers were not allowed to help her with this task.

When she got to the cottage that night, she set to work carding and spinning yarn from the down. So she went on a time, picking and carding and spinning, and all the while keeping the princes' house, cooking, and making their beds. "Goodness!" she thought, "they really are quite helpless." They came home for dinner, flapping and whirring around, and all night they were human men. But as soon as they rose in the morning, they were wild ducks again and spent their days as wild ducks do.

Now it happened once, when Snow White was out on the moor to pick thistledown (she believed it was to be for the last time!), that a young king who ruled the land was out hunting with his men, and he came riding across the moor and saw her where she stood. He paused and wondered who the lovely lass could be that was gathering thistledown. He rode up to her, "Good day to you, my lady, may I be so bold as to ask your name?"

Snow White did not say one word, but only smiled at the king. If she spoke, all hope of freeing her brothers would die. This greatly intrigued the man, and he decided at once that he would marry her. He ordered his servants to put the girl on one of the horses. Snow White struggled and wrung her hands and made all sorts of pleading gestures, pointing to her sack and then pointing to the forest from where she came.

"Obviously she wants her bags," said the king to one of his men, "take them for her."

Eventually Snow White stopped her struggles and sat quietly on her horse. The king was really a kind and handsome man, and as she heard him speak with his friends, she knew him to be thoughtful and wise as well. Slowly, she fell in love with him. She would go with him, and make him understand that she must return to help her brothers.

When they got to the king's palace, Snow White's troubles began. The old queen, who was the king's stepmother, set eyes on the beautiful young girl and her heart grew black with envy. She said to the king, "Can't you see now, that this thing, this cheap baggage whom you have picked up, and whom you are going to marry, is a witch?"

"A witch, Mother?" he laughed.

"You doubt me? Look at her, she can't talk, or laugh, or even cry. What else could she be but a witch?"

The king didn't care one fig for what his stepmother said, but held to his plans for a wedding, and he married Snow White. They lived a happy life, but the silent girl never forgot her quest. She began weaving the cloth and sewing the clothes.

She had been with her husband for almost a year when she bore him a son. The old queen was more spiteful and jealous than ever, and in the dead of night she crept into Snow White's room where she slept and stole the child. She then threw him into a pit full of vipers. She cut Snow White's finger, and smeared the blood over her mouth. Afterward she went straight to her stepson the king.

"Come quickly!" she cried. "Come see what awful creature you have wed. She has devoured her own child! Did I not tell you that she was a witch?"

The king was so heartbroken that he almost burst into tears. "It must be true, since I see it with my own eyes. But I swear she'll not do it again. I'm sure of it, so this time I will spare her life."

Before the next year was out, Snow White gave birth to another son, and the same thing happened. The king's stepmother grew more and more jealous and spiteful. She stole into the young queen's room at night, and while she slept stole the young child away. She threw him into a pit full of vipers, cut Snow White's finger, smeared the blood over her mouth, and then went and told the king that Snow White had eaten her own child. The king was so sorrowful, you can't imagine how sorry he was, and he said, "Yes, it must be true, since I see it with my own eyes; but she'll not do it again, I'm sure, and so this time too I will spare her life."

Well, before the next year was out, Snow White brought a daughter into the world, and her, too, the old queen took and threw into the pit full of vipers while the young queen slept. Then she cut Snow White's finger, smeared the blood over her mouth, and went again to the king and said, "Now you may come and see if it isn't as I say. She's wicked, wicked! The witch has gone and eaten a third babe, too."

Then the king was so sad, and saw that there was no end of it. If justice was to be done he could spare his wife no longer. He had to order her to be burnt alive on a pile of wood.

When the guards placed the young Queen Snow White near the wood-pile, she made all sorts of signs and gestures until they finally understood that she wanted to have twelve flat boards. These they gave her, and lit the pile beside her. Smoke and fire curled up all around, and they moved toward her to toss her on it, but she opened up a sack and laid out twelve pairs of neckerchiefs, and shirts, and the coats for her brothers. The youngest brother's shirt still needed its left sleeve, as she hadn't had time to finish it, but she hoped it would be enough to break the enchantment. As soon as she laid out the last of the garments, they heard such a flapping and whirring in the air, and down came twelve wild ducks flying over the forest. Each of them snapped up his clothes in his bill and flew off with them.

"See here now!" screamed the old queen to her stepson. "Wasn't I right when I told you she was a witch? Make haste and burn her before the pile burns low."

"Oh!" said the king. "We've wood enough and to spare, and so I'll wait a bit, for I have a mind to see what the end of all this will be."

As he spoke, up came the twelve princes riding along, as handsome well-grown lads as you'd wish to see, but the youngest prince had a wild duck's wing instead of his left arm.

"What's this all about?" asked the tenth brother. "Why are you going to burn our sister?"

"My queen is to be burnt because she is a witch, and because she has eaten up her own babes."

"She hasn't done any such thing," said the eleventh brother. "Speak now, sister. You have broken the troll witch's spell and you have set us free. As you saved us, now save yourself."

Then Snow White spoke, and told the whole story of how she suspected that every time she was in bed, someone had stolen into her room and taken her babes away, and cut her little finger and smeared the blood over her mouth.

"I can tell you where your babes are," said the twelfth brother. He led the party to where the snake pit was and pointed into it. There the three children were playing with the adders and vipers, and more lovely or healthy children you never saw. "The pit belongs to the trolls, and they kept our niece and nephews quite safe."

The king had them taken out at once, and went up to his stepmother, and asked what punishment she thought the woman deserved who could find it in her heart to betray a guiltless queen and three such blessed young babes.

"She deserves to be fast bound between twelve unbroken steeds so that each may take his share of her," said the old queen.

"You have spoken your own doom," said the king, "and you shall suffer it at once, for we know that it was you who tried to murder my children."

So the wicked old queen was fast bound between twelve unbroken steeds, and each got his share of her. But the king took Snow White and their three children, and her twelve brothers, and went home to his in-laws' castle. Seven years had passed since the princess had left without a word, and her parents finally learned what had happened to them all. There was joy and gladness over the whole kingdom, and the freed brothers embraced and forgave their mother. The princess had saved her twelve brothers and set them all free.

As to the brother with the one duck wing? Snow White made another journey, this time to the cabin of the troll witch. She became her apprentice, and in exchange for her service she won the enchantment that would restore her brother's arm. And when the troll witch passed on, it was Snow White who became the most powerful enchantress in the land.

The Trolls and the Pussycat

retold by Joanne Asala

There were many trolls who used to live in Brace Hill. That particular hill got its name from the villagers who put braces under the cliffs to keep the rocks from falling on the people who passed beneath them. Each day at sunset, if you were brave enough to watch, you would see the trolls marching out of their cave high up on the hill. And when the villagers tended their flocks or milked their cows, the trolls showed up on the hill and could be seen doing the same.

For most of the year the trolls kept to themselves, but each Christmas Eve they would climb down from their hilltop dwelling, go to a farm, and drive out the people as they sat at their Christmas Feast. Then they would sit down to the table and eat up all the food, and sing and dance and cause havoc far into the night.

One Christmas-time a stranger passed through the village. He had been hunting far in the north and caught a bear the likes of which had never been seen before. The bear was so large and white and fierce-looking that the hunter decided to give it as a gift to the King of Denmark. He had hoped to reach the King's palace by Christmas Eve, but the snows began to fall so thick and fast, and the winds howled so loudly, and the ice stung his face so, that he decided to seek shelter for the night.

She Covers the Whole Country, 1894-5
ARTIST: *Theodor Kittelsen*

140

The man came to a farmhouse and knocked loudly on the door; it was opened immediately by a farmer bundled in his heavy winter clothes. His family stood behind him, carrying bundles and parcels containing all of their valuables.

"May I seek shelter here for the night?" the hunter asked. "This winter storm took me by surprise, and my poor bear and myself are frozen nearly solid."

"Oh, you do not want to stay here," said the farmer. "Every Christmas Eve a pack of trolls comes down from Brace Hill to plague us. They eat our food, drink our mead, and sleep in our beds."

"And the mess that we have to clean up the next day!" his wife interrupted. "We never know for sure which farm they will invade, so we hide out in the forests until morning."

"Well, if you let me stay with my bear for the night, I do not think that you will have to hide out in the woods." The stranger convinced them that he was not afraid of the trolls, and because he seemed so brave and so strong, all of them decided to stay.

They ate a cold Christmas dinner and went to bed. The farmer's family went to sleep in their own rooms, the hunter rolled up in his blanket and slept near the hearth, and the great white bear crept under the table and was soon snoring.

But they did not sleep for long. At the stroke of midnight a terrible howling could be heard from outside, and the walls of the tiny farmhouse began to shake, and the windows began to rattle.

"Farmer Mauland! Farmer Mauland!" called a screeching, scratchy voice. "We have come for our Christmas porridge, now let us in!"

The door burst open, and in came an assortment of trolls. There were big trolls and little trolls, fat trolls and thin trolls, tall trolls and short trolls; they were the most ugly, fearsome creatures that the hunter had ever seen. They gobbled up the food that was left on the table, they broke into the cupboards and ate all the bread, and they opened up the jugs of mead and drank them down.

Suddenly one of the troll hags caught sight of the bear's tail poking out from beneath the tablecloth. "Look at the pussycat!" shouted the old hag. "The cat shall join us in our feasting. We will give the pussycat a sausage!" She stuck a fat sausage on the end of a stick, and waved it under the table.

With a grumble and a roar the huge white bear lunged out from under the table and snatched up the sausage. Then he grabbed the troll hag and threw her out the window. What a scuffle and a scrape there was! Trolls were tumbling and scrambling out the windows, they were shoving one another to get through the doorway, and leaping over the flames to go up the chimney. The next morning the hunter thanked the family for their hospitality, and continued on his journey, leading the great white bear behind him.

A year later, at Christmas-time, the farmer and his family heard the troll hag scratching at the window. "Farmer Mauland! Farmer Mauland!" she called. "Do you still have that angry cat?"

"Yes I do," said Farmer Mauland, "and this summer she had seven kittens, and we gave them to all of our neighbors."

"Then we won't dare come bother you, or any of your neighbors, ever again!"

And they never did.

Cat by Theodor Kittelsen

The Troll Who Built the Church

retold by Joanne Asala

A carpenter, whose name was Olav, was contracted to build a church at Trondheim, in Norway. But whatever his crew built during the day collapsed again at night. This made Olav very discouraged and disgusted with himself because his professional reputation was on the line, and he did not know what to do. On the third morning, when he again found the church in ruins, he fell to cursing. "What is the meaning of this?" he howled. "How can I complete the task I have promised to do?"

A short, squat little man appeared from the forest. "I can build your church for you," he said.

"You can?" The carpenter shook his head in disbelief. "If you can manage that, I'd be very surprised, very surprised, but also very grateful."

"I can build your church for you," the little man repeated, "but you must promise to give me one of three things."

"And they are?" asked Olav.

"Either the sun or the moon or your own heart."

Well, the carpenter discussed this proposal with his men. "I don't think that this little man can accomplish what all of us could not. But let's take him up on his offer. It might be good for a laugh!" So the carpenter shook hands with the ugly little man, and the bargain was sealed.

The little man started to work. The crew watched in amazement as the building was quickly constructed, but the carpenter grew more and more nervous because he realized that he would have to give the man his heart—there was no way he would ever be able to get the sun or the moon.

The little man completed his task and said, "I will release you from your bargain, if you can guess my name."

"Is it Britt? Is it Edvard? Is it Ragnar? Helmer? Jøn?" the carpenter asked hopefully.

No, it wasn't any of those names. Nor any of the others that they could come up with. "Hee, hee!" the little man chuckled with glee. "I'll be back tomorrow to collect on your debt!"

The carpenter did not wish to lose his life, and so he decided to escape. He took off in the middle of the night, and headed into the forest. He walked and he walked and he walked, and when he grew tired, he sat down near a hill.

The sound of crying voices came from within the hill, and then the voice of a tired old Trollkjerringa said, "Hush, hush, my darlings. Tonight your father Tvester will come home, and he will bring you the sun, the moon or perhaps the heart of the village carpenter."

What wonderful news that was to the carpenter's ears! He rushed back home, and on the way home he met the little man, whom he now realized was a troll.

"You want me to give you my heart," he said, "but what will you use it for?"

"To season my children's soup," the troll said. "But you can still go free if you can guess my name."

"Is it Ole? Is it Carl? Hans? No? Well, then it has to be Tvester."

"What?!?!?!" the troll shouted in disbelief. "Who told you? *Who told you?*" The troll got so mad that he tore a path through the forest; he knocked over trees and dug up bushes, he pushed over boulders and ripped up the flowers. By the time he got to the church, he tore out a stone from the east side. He wanted to tear down the whole church, but could not. To this day the villagers say that the stone will not stay in place.

The Ash Lad Who Had an Eating Match with the Troll, 1883
ARTIST: *Theodor Kittelsen*

The Ash Lad Who Had an Eating Match with the Troll

by Jørgen Moe
translated by George Webbe Dasent

There was once a farmer who had three sons; his means were small, he was old and feeble, and his sons wouldn't turn their hands to a thing. A large, vast forest belonged to the farm, and one day the father asked his sons to go and chop wood to try to pay off some of their debts.

Well, after much cajoling, the farmer convinced his oldest son to go first. But when he had gotten far into the forest, and began to hew at a shaggy old fir, what should he see coming up to him but a big, burly troll! "If you chop down the trees in my forest, I'll kill you," he said.

When the lad heard that, he flung aside his axe, and ran off toward home as fast as he could lay legs to the ground. Quite out of breath, he told his father what had happened. "You are a hare-heart," the old man said. "No troll would have ever scared me from hewing trees when I was young."

So the next day the second son's turn came, and he fared the same as his brother. He had hardly struck the shaggy fir tree three times when the troll came to him too, and said, "If you hew trees in this wood of mine, I'll kill you."

Like his older brother, the second son threw down his axe and beat a path for home. When he arrived, his father was very angry, and said that no troll had ever scared him when he was young.

On the third day, Boots wanted to set off.

"You?" asked the older brothers. "Indeed! You'll do it bravely, no doubt—you who've never been beyond the front door!"

Boots ignored his brothers' cruel teasing, and simply asked for a good store of food. Since his mother had no cheese curds, he hung a pot over the fire to make himself some, put the curds into his knapsack, and set off into the forest.

After chopping awhile, Boots saw the troll come up to him. "If you chop the trees in my forest, I'll kill you," said the troll.

But Boots was clever; he pulled his cheese out of the knapsack, and squeezed it till the whey spurted out.

"Watch your tongue and mind your manners!" he cried to the troll. "Or I'll squeeze you like I'm squeezing the water out of this white stone!"

The terrified troll quickly backed down, "No! Don't hurt me! If you spare my life, I'll help you chop wood."

"Well...." Boots pretended to think the matter over. "I suppose that I can strike that bargain." The troll helped Boots chop down the trees, and by nightfall they had several cords of wood.

When evening drew near, the troll said, "My home is closer than yours, you'd better come back with me."

Boots was willing enough, and when they reached the troll's home, the troll made up the fire, while the lad went to fetch water for their porridge. Two iron pails stood by the fireplace, and they were so big and heavy, that he couldn't so much as lift them from the ground, much less get them to the well to fill with water.

"Bah!" said Boots. "It's not worth my while to touch these finger bowls. I'll just go and fetch the spring itself."

"No, no, my friend," said the troll. "I can't afford to lose my spring water; just you make up the fire, and I'll go get the water."

When the troll got back, they cooked a large pot of porridge.

"Let's have an eating match," the lad challenged the troll. The huge troll eagerly agreed; he knew he could hold his own in any eating match. So they sat down, but the lad took his knapsack unawares to the troll, and hung it before him, and so he spooned more into the scrip than he ate himself; and when it was full, he took up his knife and made a slit in the scrip. The troll watched all the while, but never said a word. When they had eaten a while longer, the troll laid down his spoon, saying, "No! I can't eat a morsel more!"

"You must eat," encouraged the lad. "I'm not even half-full yet. Do as I did and cut a hole in your stomach so you can keep eating as much as you want!"

"But doesn't it hurt you cruelly?"

"Nothing to speak of," said the lad.

So the troll cut a gash in his hairy belly and, of course, he died. The boy gathered up all of the gold and silver that he found in the hillside, and went home with it, and you may be glad to hear that it went a great way to pay off the debt.

The Troll Turned Cat

by Thomas Keightly

About a quarter of a mile from Sorøe lies Pedersborg, and a little farther on is the town of Lyng. Just between these towns is a hill called Brøndhøi, said to be inhabited by the Troll People.

There goes a story that there was once among these Troll People of Brøndhøi an old cross-grained curmudgeon of a troll, whom the rest nicknamed Knurremurre (Rumble-Mumble) because he was evermore the cause of noise and uproar within the hill. This Knurremurre, having discovered what he thought to be too great a degree of intimacy between his young wife and a young troll of the society, took this in such ill part that he vowed vengeance, swearing he would have the life of the young one. The latter, accordingly, thought it would be his best course to be off out of the hill 'til better times; so turning himself into a noble tortoiseshell tomcat, he left his old residence, and journeyed down to the neighboring town of Lyng, where he established himself in the house of an honest poor man named Plat.

Here he lived for a long time comfortable and easy, with nothing to annoy him, and was as happy as any tomcat or troll crossed in love well could be. He got every day plenty of milk and good groute to eat, and lay the whole day long at his ease in a warm armchair behind the stove.

Plat happened one evening to come home rather late, and as he entered the room the cat was sitting in his usual place, scraping meal groute out of a pot, and licking the pot itself carefully. "Harkye, dame," called Plat to his wife as he came in at the door, "'til I tell you what happened to me on the road. Just as I was coming past Brøndhøi, there came out a troll, and he called out to me, and said, 'Harkye Plat, tell your cat, that Knurremurre is dead!'"

The moment the cat heard these words, he tumbled the pot down on the floor, sprang out of the chair, and stood up on his hind legs. Then, as he hurried out of the door, he cried out with exultation, "What! Is Knurremurre dead? Then I may go home as fast as I please!" And so saying, he scampered off to the hill, to the amazement of the honest Plat, and it is likely he lost no time in making his advances on the young widow.

A Farmer Tricks a Troll

by Thomas Keightly

A farmer, on whose ground there was a little hill, resolved not to let it lie idle, so he began at one end to plough it up. The hill man, who lived in it, came to him and said, "How dare you plough on the roof of my house!"

"I assure you," said the farmer, "that I did not know that this was your house. But I must say that it is equally unprofitable to us both to let such a fine piece of land lie idle. Therefore I suggest we make a deal."

"A deal?" asked the troll suspiciously. "What kind of deal?"

"Well, I suggest you let me plough, sow, and reap this piece of land every year on these terms: that we should take it year and year about, and you shall one year have what grew on the ground and I what grew in the ground, and the next year I shall have what grew on the ground, and you what grew in it. Deal?"

"Deal!" said the troll, quite satisfied with the bargain.

The agreement was made accordingly, but the crafty farmer took care to sow carrots and corn year and year about, and he gave the hill man the tops of the carrots and the roots of the corn for his share, with which he was well-content. They thus lived for a long time on extremely good terms with each other.

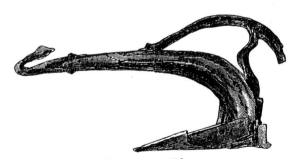

Norwegian Plow

PART TWO: *The New World*

Leaving behind the old problems

From "The Troll," retold by Andrew Lang, 1900
ARTIST: *H.J. Ford*

Journey to the New World

by Joanne Asala and Joan Liffring-Zug Bourret

When the Norwegians first sailed to North America, they left the trolls at home. Who would want to take such ugly, enormous, smelly creatures along anyway? Besides, on a small sailing ship or a Viking boat, there would not have been room. Some trolls were as big as mountains! People seeking new worlds want to leave all unpleasant acquaintances back at home.

The first Norwegians who came over were the Vikings. It was a seafaring Viking named Eirik the Red who traveled with his father to Iceland. We do not know for sure why he was called "the Red." Was it his red face? His red hair? Perhaps it was the blood he spilled in battle. In any case, he continued his explorations from Iceland, and brought his people to Greenland.

Leif Eirikson, the son of Eirik the Red, gathered another group of men and continued to travel out into the unknown. Eventually they landed in a place they called "Vinland the Good," on a continent we know as North America. This was five hundred years before Christopher Columbus made his historic voyage. Today, various organizations are dedicated to spreading the word about Leif Eirikson's discovery, and they have erected statues of him on both coasts. But did Eirik or Leif bring trolls with them to share in their discoveries? Of course not. At least, no mention of them has been made in the sagas.

The next boatload of Norwegians certainly didn't have room for any trolls either, and would have been horrified at the suggestion that they bring such creatures to the New World. This second group of people came to America in 1825 on the ship *The Restauration.* The fifty-two men, women, and children on the ship not only had to suffer the misery of a cramped ocean voyage, but they were held in detention by authorities because there were too many of them on the ship. Ultimately they were allowed to disembark, and they were the beginning of what was to become one of the largest European immigrations. In all, over 800,000 people came from Norway to America between the years of 1820 and 1990. Not one of them smuggled a troll into his baggage.

The people of Norway who came to America were seeking the opportunity to own land and to have a more plentiful life. For centuries the Norwegian farmers had been freemen with the oldest son inheriting the farm. But a mountainous country is short of good land for farming, and there were few prospects for the younger sons and daughters. Letters sent back home proclaimed America as the promised land, so many left to seek their fortune.

Nothing, however, was promised to the trolls. The trolls were all left behind in the Old World, and there they stayed until the end of World War II. For over 150 years, Norwegian immigrants did not give a thought to the needs of any trolls because for over a thousand years the trolls had given everyone they came across a lot of trouble.

Trolls were large, ugly creatures of extreme selfishness. They were the epitome of evil. They had tails and cunning minds and were a problem to the good farmers and fishermen of Norway. Trolls existed in the minds of the people prior to Christianity. When Christianity was forced by threat of death upon all of Scandinavia in the eleventh century, trolls and the old Norse Gods were banished and existed only in the tales people told on long winter evenings or under the summer stars while they slept in their *sæter* (a *sæter* is a mountain hut where the young spent the summers with the grazing herds of cattle).

A new era began to dawn for trolls in the mid 1800s. That was when the fairy tales of Norway were published with the drawings of Erik Werenskiold and Theodor Kittelsen. But there was still a half-century waiting period as trolls evolved and stopped causing all kinds of trouble, and began to smell better.

It was after World War II that artists, craftsmen, and manufacturers began creating replicas of the trolls of old. Importers sponsored a massive troll immigration to America. While these trolls are not coming for a better life or to own a farm or to terrify the children, they do want homes. Americans by the thousands, if not millions, are offering their customary generous hospitality to these new arrivals. There are no signs of a diminishing of the waves of trolls coming. But these are not the same creatures that terrified Norwegian children. If the trolls had not changed their behavior and, to some extent, their appearance, they could never have cleared customs and immigration. As Vivian Bergquist of Bergquist Imports, Inc. says, "You must fully realize that we cannot sell ugly, mean trolls. Ugly is one thing, but mean is quite another. Our trolls have cleaned up their act in order to get visas to come to the U.S. They are quite happy here and are fairly clean-living except for a few bouts of mischief now and then."

Americans are voluntarily paying for their passage here every time a troll finds a home or a site to stand. Other trolls are being created in America in school workshops out of papier maché, mass-produced in factories, or hand-crafted for art fairs. Homes for them seem increasingly easier to find.

While many of the Norwegian trolls of yesterday were horribly ugly creatures, trolls today vary in appearance. Norwegian artists have evolved trolls that are more lovable and appealing.

Other trolls are still extremely ugly. One analyst of the phenomenon of troll immigration says, "The uglier the better. People have a need to own something that is extremely ugly and has human characteristics. Maybe having a grotesque two-and-a-half-foot troll is a rebellion against the advertising standards of what is beautiful in our culture. Not everyone wants to bring home a mannequin to live by the mantle or in the yard as part of the garden decoration or even as a doorstop."

With understanding may come love, even for the extremely ugly.

Fifth Generation American Trolls of Norwegian Descent

153

Making a Troll of Your Own

by Judith Simundson

Papier Maché Mash

16 pages of newspaper or newsprint*
2 cups water
1/4 cup white glue
2 tablespoons whiting
   (available in craft stores or from stained glass suppliers)
1 tablespoon linseed oil (or a bit more)
a few drops wintergreen oil or clove oil
   (wintergreen oil is available at pharmacies)

1. Tear the newspaper into small pieces about one to two inches in size. Soak in water overnight.

2. Blend a small handful of the wet paper with two or more cups water in a blender for about 30 seconds, or until the fibers are totally broken.

3. Pour into a strainer to remove excess water.

4. Repeat steps 1–3 until all the paper is blended and strained.

5. Discard excess water standing in the blended paper, but *do not squeeze dry*. Yields about one quart of blended paper.

6. Add glue, whiting, linseed oil, and wintergreen oil. Use your fingers to assure a thorough mixing.

* Printed newspaper will give a gray mash. Unprinted newsprint will create a buff-colored mash. Mash renders a rough texture. Halfway through the drying process you can smooth the surface with a knife, burnisher, or your fingers. Even with smoothing, it will be rougher than clay—very appropriate for trolls!

To Create A Small Troll

A small figure can be made of solid mash. Insert sticks or toothpicks between joints for greater stability. (Example: a toothpick between the head and the body, from body to arm, etc.) Use a toothpick or small knife to carve detail into the figure.

Medium Troll

Large figures require a mold or armature and additional newspaper or newsprint and white glue.

1. One way to make a medium-sized figure is to put a plastic bag or plastic wrap over a doll.

2. Dip newspaper strips into the wet mash and overlay the plastic-wrapped doll's face with the strips, brushing on white glue between each layer of newspaper. For details, mold the mash directly over the newspaper strips using glue on the newspaper and adding more glue with each addition of mash. Water will run off the face and pool below. After drying a few hours, you can begin molding the face in greater detail.

3. When the face is fairly dry, remove the doll carefully. Cover the papier maché face with plastic wrap and place nose-down into sand or flour, with plastic wrap between the face and the flour. Place a small blown-up balloon on the face back. Begin adding papier maché mash from the edges of the face and around the back of the head. After drying a few hours you can begin molding the face in greater detail. Each time you add mash, use a touch of glue to bond the new mash to the drier mash.

4. Extend the neck and provide shoulders so the clothing can hang from the shoulders.

5. Pop the balloon when the troll head is dry and gently pull the balloon free.

Troll Head in a Balloon

Large Troll

If you are making a large figure, your mold can be of chicken wire or screen roughly shaped like a troll and wired together to be self-supporting.

Layer strips of glue-wet newspaper over wire using the white glue between each layer of newspaper. Use one or two layers of newspaper. You may wish to let each layer dry before adding more newspaper. This assures that the whole piece will be dry throughout. Also, the dried layers are more stiff and supportive of subsequent layers. For details, mold mash over glue-covered newspaper.

Painting

When the troll is completely dry, paint with artists' oil paints. Oil paint gives the troll greater durability and hardness. Load the paint brush with linseed oil and frost the tip with paint. Drag the color into every crack and use additional linseed oil to drag the color out and away. This softens each crease and gives natural shading.

Optional: Spray the painted troll with several coats of polyurethane varnish, allowing each coat to dry before applying the next.

Troll Emerging in Chicken Wire

American Garden Troll with Norwegian Ancestry
ARTIST: *Diane Heusinkveld*

What to Do if a Troll Finds You!

A Short List of Precautions

If you have to go walking alone along some deserted road at night, always keep a cross, Bible, or steel object in hand. This will not only protect you from trolls, but will keep you from being afraid. If you do see a troll, recite *The Lord's Prayer* or the twenty-third psalm.

Ringing bells (particularly church bells), firing rifles, or banging on pots and pans will usually make trolls scatter; they can't stand loud noises.

Check for a cow's tail peeking out from under the skirts of strange women you meet.

Carefully avoid trees, clumps of bushes, dark shadows, mountains, rocks, or any object that looks like a troll—it just might be one!

Be cautious when you meet unruly children, giant white bears, cute pussy cats, beautiful princesses, or strange horses. They may be trolls in disguise.

Don't brag about what you'd do if you saw a troll, or one will surely find you!

Troll Pudding

Christmas Rømmegrøt for Your Local Nisse

1 quart cream (not too fresh)	3/4 quart milk
1 cup flour (more if needed)	sugar and salt to taste

Stirring constantly, bring cream to a full boil until foam is gone. Add flour gradually to make a thick mush. Stir until butter appears. Remove butter and reserve. Bring milk to a boil. Add hot milk gradually to mush, stirring constantly. Simmer 10 to 20 minutes, stirring frequently until mixture thickens. Add sugar and salt to taste. Don't forget to top with reserved butter, or who knows how the Nisse will react!

Select List of Resources

and Recommended Readings

Asbjørnsen, Peter Christian; Moe, Jørgen. George W. Dasent, Translator. *Popular Tales from the Norse*, Edinburgh, 1888.

Asbjørnsen, Peter Christian. *Tales from the Fjeld*. Chapman and Hill, London, 1874.

Asbjørnsen, Peter Christian; H. L. Braekstad, Translator. *Round the Yule Log*. London, 1881.

Asbjørnsen, Peter Christian; Moe, Jørgen. Joan Roll-Hansen, Translator. *A Time for Trolls*. Oslo, 1962.

Asbjørnsen, Peter Christian; Moe, Jørgen. *Eventyrbog for Børn*. Copenhagen, 1883.

Asbjørnsen, Peter Christian; Moe, Jørgen. *Samlede Eventyr*. Gyldendal Norsk Forlag, Oslo, 1883.

Asbjørnsen, Peter Christian; Moe, Jørgen. *Udvalgte Folkeeventyr*. Kristiania, 1907.

Ekstrand, Florence. *Norwegian Trolls and Other Tales*. Welcome Press, Seattle, 1990.

Fiske, Arland O. *The Scandinavian World*. North American Heritage Press, Minot, North Dakota, 1988.

Hofberg, Herman; W.H. Meyers, Translator. *Swedish Fairy Tales*. 1895.

Jonsen, George. *Favorite Tales of Monsters and Trolls*. Random House, New York, 1977.

Ketilsson, Eli. *Troll*. Stenersens Forlag, Oslo, 1989.

Ketilsson, Eli. *Norway: Home of the Trolls*. Medusa, Jar, Norway, 1993.

Kittelsen, Theodor. *Troldskab*. Kristiania, 1892.

Lie, Jonas; R. Nisbet Bain, Translator. *Weird Tales from the Northern Seas*, 1893.

Østby, Leif. *Theodor Kittelsen: Tegninger og akvareller*. Dreyers Forlag, Oslo, 1975.

Stavig, Art. *Trolls, Trolls, Trolls*. Pine Hill Press, Freeman, South Dakota, 1979.

Norwegian-American Troll Covered with Grass Clippings
ARTIST: *Diane Heusinkveld*